OAKLAND COMMUNITY COLLEGE
3 2355 00152590 6

T4-AUB-924

A Later Son, a Different Daughter

A Later Son, a Different Daughter

by Harry Atkins

McGraw-Hill Book Company
New York Toronto London Sydney

A LATER SON, A DIFFERENT DAUGHTER

Library of Congress Catalog Card Number: 68-13621

First Edition 00738

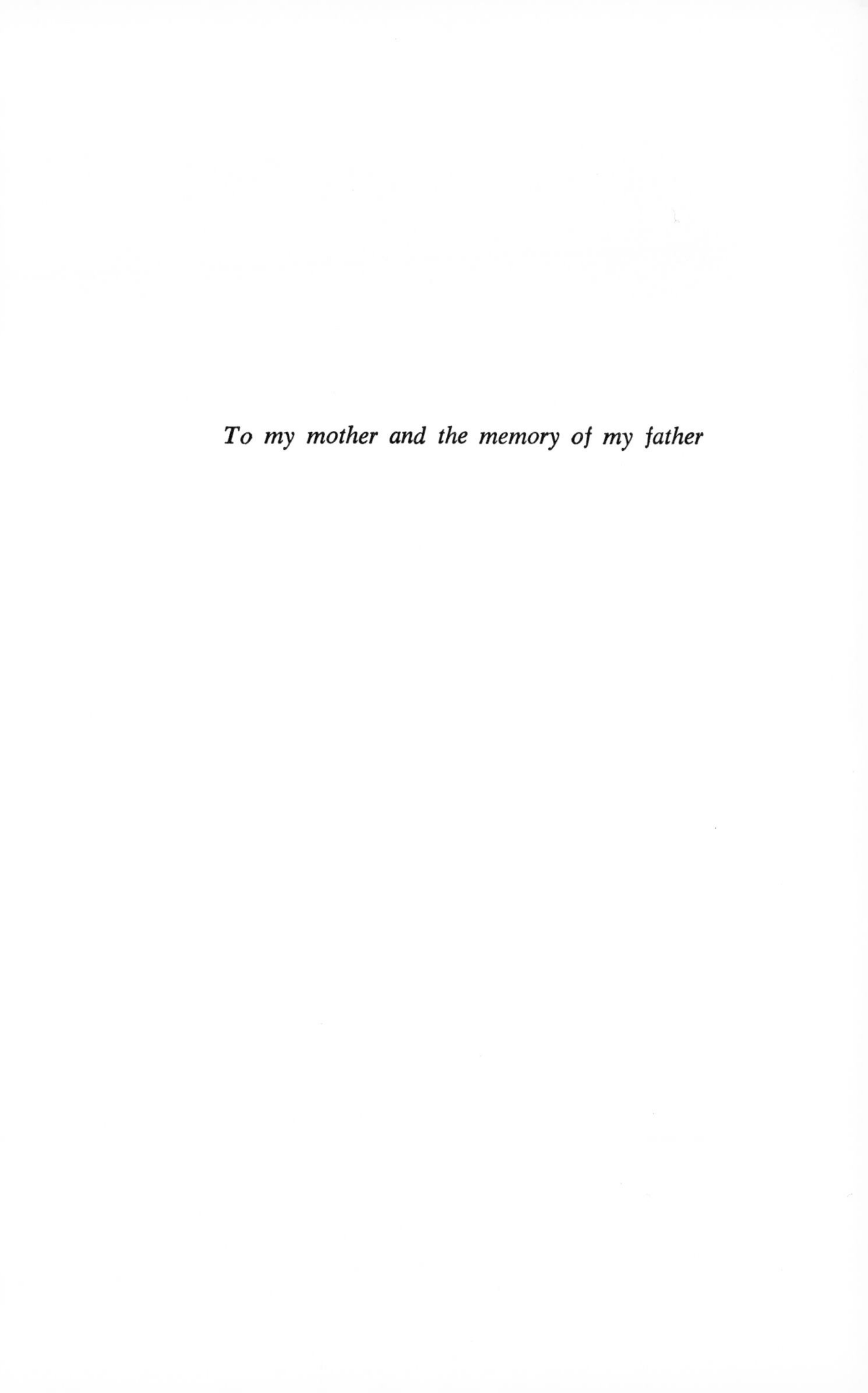

To my mother and the memory of my father

". . . as if it came back, as if life came back,
Not in a later son, a different daughter, another place,
But as if evening found us young, still young,
Still walking in a present of our own."

WALLACE STEVENS

A Later Son, a Different Daughter

Part One

FROM SAN ANTONIO the highway shoots one hundred and fifty-eight miles to the border, straight through the middle of the desert and the middle of the sun, and a silver Greyhound can make the trip in a little more than two hours. You can make good time on that road, but you have to be careful in the summer because the heat waves simmering up out of the macadam make the whole road sizzle and float until it doesn't seem like a road at all, but a wavy transparent river hovering just above the ground.

And if you're not used to that kind of driving you keep thinking you're going to head into a black puddle a mile ahead and you keep watching to see if it gets any nearer. You keep watching it and you forget about anything but watching that puddle, and then you're in the sand or tangled up in a patch of scrub.

But if you're used to that kind of driving you know enough to shift your eyes from one side of the highway to the other and not stare straight down the center.

It's a long trip and it seems longer than it is because you never can be really certain you are moving forward at all. The dead land stays dead, and who is to say that the strangled bushes and half-buried sagebrush cages are not the same ones you have passed before and are merely passing again. You *are* moving, of course, and it is only that the sun has burned life out of every mile, leaving no comparisons along the way, leaving you to rely for a sense of movement upon the whine of your tires on the blacktop and the bright splashes of blood which cake in star-like patterns on your windshield.

And if you stop for gasoline or to rest, it's on the edge of towns like Bracksville or Urando or Hargrett, at roadside stands where over the sandy railroad embankment and the bright streak of track you see the sun-faded brick of a Baptist church or the glint of metal from a used-car lot.

They appear suddenly, these towns, with no more warning than a few frame houses strung out three or four miles apart along the highway—bleached wooden boxes perched out there on a patch of naked red clay cleared out of the pygmy scrub that stretches all the way to the horizon, tough and spiny as chicken feet, and you may wonder about these houses on the outskirts of towns which themselves seem no more than outskirts of existence—farms with no farmland, ranches with no livestock, now sitting unprotected along the highway.

But they were not always this isolated, for as you drive you see rotted timbers and charred foundations of other houses which once formed links to the towns. As you speed by the ones still standing you catch a glimpse of a figure on the porch or someone disappearing behind the corner of a building and you wonder why the sun does not eat into the slats of these houses until they burst into a shower of splinters.

But after you have seen a few and wondered about them, the rest hold little interest. Mostly the houses look the same.

Except that in front of the Shaylors' house near Hargrett there is a tree, a live oak that Margaret Shaylor had planted ten years ago when they had moved from the other house, and which she had kept alive with two saucepans of kitchen tap water every day, carrying one out to the tree in the morning before Jesse and the children were up, and one in the evening just after dark. And now, though the brittle crust of earth had thickened and under an inch of loose soil was beginning to choke the roots, the live oak still got no more than two splashes of water from Margaret's kitchen tap. The spring rains had come and gone, staying less time than the year before, and on the branches that leaned into the front porch, leaves that had managed to hatch from buds already had become brown and dry. The squat five-room house that Jesse and Howard had whitewashed the summer before was beginning to flake.

At eleven o'clock Saturday morning it was ninety-two degrees, and in the middle of the yard in front of the house, Jesse's boots stuck out from under the body of the Ford pick-up while Howard leaned against the front fender, squinting across the highway. Howard was twenty-one, tall and loose-limbed with a narrow face rescued from mulishness by deep-set eyes the same faded blue as the eleven o'clock sky. His hair was only a shade darker than the sandy topsoil. During the hour he had been out in the yard with his father he had not moved from the fender. There was no trace of sweat on his forehead, and his white T-shirt was still fresh and unwrinkled. If he heard the heavy breathing and clanking of metal that came from under the truck he made no sign, nor seemed to notice the buzzing of the giant grasshoppers that ricocheted off the hood. Only his fingers moved, tapping a slow rhythm on the seams of his starched khakis.

"Howie? You still up there?" His father's voice was muffled under the truck. "You want to hand me a three-eighths out of that box in the cab?" Howard didn't answer. "Howie! Goddammit, you still up there? I'm asking you to get me a three-eighths!"

Howard blinked. "What do you need, a wrench?"

"Make it a five-eighths; the brake shoe's loose. No, give me the whole damn toolbox. I'll need a screwdriver and pliers too."

Howard rubbed his knuckles along the rusty fender. "Well, do you need anything else? Because if you don't I'll just hand you those instead of dragging out the whole box." He waited a few seconds for an answer, then pulled the box out from under the seat, carried it around to the other side of the truck and slid it in next to where his father lay on his back. He went back around to the fender, settled himself against it and looked out at the highway again. But this time he listened to his father rummaging through the toolbox and he waited.

"Now let's see . . ." his father began after a while, and

Howard traced a line in the dust with his toe. "Up there kind of looking over the lay of the land, are you?" He sounded preoccupied and Howard pictured him fitting the wrench to a bolt as he spoke. "Well that's all right, Howie. That's not a bad thing for somebody to be doing. I used to do it myself once in a while when I was your age. Ah goddammit!" The wrench struck brightly against metal. "There's nothing wrong in that. You'll never hear me say you can't learn a lot from just standing around looking at the sky and figuring things out. Understand what I mean, Howie? You still up there?"

"I'm still here."

"But the thing is . . ." His father's heels had gouged two half moons in the ground. ". . . I don't believe that's all there is to it. Because that's not *all* I did when I was your age. I mean, I don't believe also that I was working behind the counter of a drugstore when I was twenty-one." A tool clanked into the box. "If I remember correctly . . ."

Howard stood up straight. "You already had fifteen head of cattle by then," he said in an even voice. "You were wrangling outside of Creighton and putting all your money back into livestock, weren't you?"

"*Seven*teen head," his father answered. A moment later he was standing on the other side of the truck, brushing dust off his shirt and the seat of his coveralls and facing his son across the hood. Sweat coated his forehead and glistened in the gray stubble of his chin and jaw. Jesse Shaylor had the same narrow build as his son, and the years had added little extra flesh, so that at fifty-eight, while his shoulders were slightly rounded, his body was as tight and hard as when he had slept on ranges with only a saddle blanket between him and the baked earth. And in his face you could see Howard's face—the high cheekbones, the wide mouth, the prominent chin, though the lines of a perpetual frown, as yet only suggested in the son, were deeply etched into the father's brow.

"And I know what you're thinking," Shaylor said, fastening the latch on the toolbox; "that that was a long time ago and I might have had 'em then but I don't have 'em now, and that you might be just working behind the counter at Kearney's, but *I'm* only working at Boyd McHenry's garage, and it don't matter a damn what I had then because I don't have a goddam bit more than this to show for it now." Shaylor's backhand gesture included the house, the lean-to shed and the rusty skeleton of a tractor that lay on its back at one edge of the yard.

"I didn't say I was thinking that."

"No? Well you see it don't even matter that much—that I lost it all. Because everything I brought in, everything I ever got, I got by myself with not any help from anybody, and when it wasn't there any more it wasn't that I let it get away, it was *taken* away. It was taken away by the land. And I don't believe there's much you can do when the land takes things away. I believe you can't do a lot more than sit and watch and maybe hope for it to rain."

Howard put his hands in his back pockets and turned so he was facing the highway again. "That was when your ranchland dried up on you."

"Dried up? I guess it did. I guess it sure goddam well dried up on me and every other grassland livestock rancher around. Except it didn't seem to dry up so fast for the ones who weren't out there in the sun working their own stock on forty or fifty acres. It didn't dry up for the ones with five or ten thousand head and land you couldn't drive around in less than a day, because it don't much matter if there's water or not if you can drill all the way to the center of the earth, or pick up a telephone and order a couple of hundred boxcars-full of rain from Kansas City or St. Louis."

Howard kicked a stone. "They pipe it now."

"And I'm working in Boyd McHenry's garage now." He brought the toolbox around and slid it under the seat, then leaned back against the cab and lit a cigarette. Out on the highway the Laredo bus raced by scattering earth and gravel along the road shoulders, and for an instant a dozen soft green faces were turned toward the house.

They watched the bus grow smaller, and when it was out of sight Shaylor stepped on the cigarette. "But if you think that's an excuse, it's not and I don't mean it to be, even though there's a couple of hundred men in this town alone, working for National Oil or working somebody else's land, who'll use it as an excuse, and nobody including me will think the less of 'em."

Without looking, Howard reached out and slammed the truck door. "If we're all going into town with Laura I guess I better go in and get washed up." Howard turned away from his father and headed toward the house, and then, even before it touched him, felt his father's hand on his shoulder, spinning him around so fast that he had difficulty keeping his balance.

"What are *you* planning to use for an excuse, Howie? You settled on one yet or are you still looking around for one you like the sound of?"

Howard shrugged off the hand and backed away a couple of steps. "All right, all right."

Shaylor hooked his thumbs into his belt. "That's nice; it's real fine that you think it's all right because that takes care of everything, don't it?" He took a flannel rag from his back pocket and mopped his face and neck. "It's just too bad you're not what's-his-name, Walt Pendleton's boy, the one that can't talk straight. A boy like that got a pretty good built-in excuse, going through his whole life doing nothing but wrapping bundles and no one looking to him for anything else, in fact giving him a lot of credit just for doing what he is. That the kind of thing you're looking for? Except it might be tougher for you because a lot of people know you're a little smarter than Pendleton's boy; a lot of people might think that somebody three years out of high school ought to be doing something besides working in a drugstore. I mean, *Laura* graduates today, and chances are even she'll be doing something better than that."

Howard let his breath out slowly through his teeth. "All right, then what do you want? Do you want me to pack up and get out of here, is that it? Does it make you nervous to have me hanging around? Okay, I can do that; I can do that without any trouble if you're all that worried about my working at Kearney's. Maybe I've got some plans you don't even know about, but if you don't want me here, if you don't want me to stay in this house any more, that's okay with me because I can go right now, right this minute." His voice trailed off and he felt in his pockets for cigarettes. There were dark spots on his T-shirt where it was sticking to his chest.

Shaylor turned away and looked out at the road, and when he spoke again it was without sarcasm. "I'm not asking you to leave my house or anything like that, Howie. I'm just asking you to do something, *something,* even if it doesn't work out. That's all." On the other side of the highway a yellow jackrabbit was creeping along the gravel shoulder. It stopped, tiptoed halfway across the blacktop, then sat poised on its haunches, nose twitching.

"Did you ever think," Howard said slowly, "that even working at Kearney's might be 'something'? And I don't mean forever; I don't mean I'm planning to stay there forever. I'm talking about now, and I don't see what's so wrong about it."

His father waited a moment before answering. "If I thought that was it, if I thought you had some plans in your mind beyond that drugstore, I wouldn't be saying all this. But I don't really believe you do. I'm not even trying to give you a lecture, Howie, but it's been two *years* you been there and I just can't help thinking that when I was your age . . ."

Howard flipped his cigarette away. "Yeah, I know, but I thought we were talking about *me*. I mean, we've been over that a couple of times and I guess I know pretty well what you were doing then and what you're doing now."

Shaylor's hand went to his mouth.

"I didn't mean it that way," Howard said quickly. "That's not what I was trying to say."

They stood there, facing each other, and then from the porch, Margaret Shaylor's soft voice reached them. "You two better hurry up out there. There's not much time. I'm putting lunch on the table in about half an hour."

"We're coming," Shaylor said over his shoulder. The screen door banged shut and Howard started for the house; after he had watched a giant trailer truck roar south down the highway, Shaylor followed him.

When Shaylor came into the kitchen Howard was not there, and if he had let his mother know about the conversation in the yard there was no telling from the way Margaret, her arms buried to the elbows in suds, looked up from the sink to smile as the door slammed. "You better hurry and get washed up, Jess. We've only got an hour and a half before the graduation, and lunch'll be ready as soon as you get out of the shower."

Shaylor stood in the middle of the kitchen. Upstairs, Laura was singing over the rush of the shower. He listened for a moment, then stepped into the back hall. "You planning to use up all the damn hot water, Laura?" he shouted. "You might take into account there's others of us wanting to get in there!" The singing stopped abruptly, and seconds later the water was turned off. Shaylor came back into the kitchen. "You'd think that goddam shower was put in just for her own private use." He went to the cabinet above the icebox and got out the bottle of sour mash Boyd had given him last Easter. "That'll be it for the hot water, you can be sure of that."

Margaret looked at him over her shoulder. "What's the matter, Jess, couldn't you get the truck fixed?" She pulled out the plug and wiped her arms on a dishtowel. Shaylor sat down at the kitchen table and rubbed his knuckles along the edge where the porcelain had worn away to a black border.

"Well," he said, "I fixed it. There wasn't much to fixing it." Margaret untied her apron and flounced the skirt of her blue dirndl and patted her hair where it was pulled back and fastened in a bun. She walked over and stood behind her husband and put her hands on his shoulders. There were droplets of moisture on her forehead and her face was flushed from standing over the sink, but she was still a pretty woman whose face, though soft and florid, was free of wrinkles, as if she had somehow absorbed the same experiences that had left their mark so visibly on her husband. "What's the trouble then, Jess? What's on your mind?"

Shaylor finished the whisky and stood up. "Well," he said, toying with the glass, "nothing."

"We ought to be in there by quarter-after-one if we want to get a good seat."

He walked into the back hall, then turned in the doorway. "I *did* get off to a fast start though, didn't I, Maggie? Anyone would have to admit that." He disappeared. For several seconds Margaret stood by his chair, then took silverware from the counter and began setting the table.

Upstairs, Howard was fixing his necktie in the bathroom mirror. "No more hot water!" he called out as his father passed. "Laura used it all up; spent the whole morning in the shower. You want me to heat some shaving water for you?"

"No, I don't want that, I guess I've shaved with cold before."

Howard tugged on the strands of his tie to even up the points.

"I know, but what about a shower?"

"A cold shower never hurt anybody either," Shaylor said from the end of the hallway.

Howard took a last look, then followed his father into the bedroom and sat on the edge of the bed. "No, I guess it never did. It's not *too* cold anyway, not ice cold. As a matter of fact, it's only a little below body temperature, so it wouldn't be so bad." Shaylor slipped down the suspenders of his coveralls, took off his denim work shirt and tossed it in a corner behind the laminated maple bureau. "I figured I wouldn't bother with a shower myself," Howard added. He watched his father scratch himself under the armpits. "Anyway, I thought that after Laura graduates you all might come over to Kearney's for a soda. I'm going to have to go over there right away after the ceremonies to get to work, but I won't be too busy by the time you get there, and I figured we could all sit in a booth."

"It's all right with me if it's all right with Laura and your mother." Shaylor was looking over Howard's head, above the bed where on the pink wall was tacked a large piece of cowhide, tanned to burnt umber and cut into the shape of the state of Texas. He looked down at his son. "About what I was saying out in the yard . . ."

Howard got up quickly and went to the front window. "Oh well, that's all right. I guess I was just probably getting on your nerves, standing around while you were under the truck working. Tomorrow I'll take a good look at it myself; maybe check the brake shoe again and the springs and everything like that."

Shaylor stood there in his coveralls, the suspenders dangling to his knees, his arms folded across his chest. "You think that's it do you, Howie? You think I was worried about you not helping me with the truck?"

"No, I mean it," Howard said, turning away from the window. "I'm not doing anything special tomorrow, and it's a long time since I gave it a good checking over."

"All right," Shaylor said. "All right."

"But there was one thing I *was* wondering about." Howard turned back to the window and looked out. "About what you were saying out in the yard . . ." He heard his father's boots hit the floor. "Those men you were talking about—I mean men like Cal Watson and Veatus Price and Bart Supler and Tyler Prentiss. All of them had something of their own going for them once, didn't they? Isn't that what you were telling me? Well, before they lost it, before it was taken away from them, how did they act? Did they change a lot when they had to go to work for somebody else, I mean change in the way they thought about things? You see, the men I'm talking about are good men, and I was just wondering . . ." Howard turned away from the window and saw that his father had left the room, might even have left just after he had started to speak, after he had heard the boots drop. He leaned back against the window and looked around the room at the crumpled shirt on the floor, the boots slanted away from each other at an impossible angle, his mother's pink hat nesting on the doorknob. In a moment he heard the bright hiss of the shower. He went into the hall and stood in front of the bathroom door.

"Those men I'm thinking about are good men," he said loudly. He waited, then lowered his voice. "I remember one time about three years ago seeing Tyler Prentiss on the corner near the courthouse. He was just leaning against a mailbox, and I remember thinking it'd be a lot of big men you'd have to see before you found one that handled himself like Tyler, standing there as if the whole town of Hargrett was something he'd built singlehanded. And then, a little later, walking home, I remembered Tyler worked behind the counter at old man Temple's hardware store, and anyone could go in anytime and tell him they wanted something, and watch him skitter and poke behind the counter, trying to come up with the screwdriver or doorlatch they were looking for."

The shower stopped and Howard listened to the house creak, hearing his mother moving about in the kitchen. He went back and stood in the doorway of the bedroom and looked in. "And now it's now, and all the big men like Tyler and Cal and you—it's you I'm talking about, Papa—had something taken away and can't get it back." He walked over to the center of the room and moved the boots with his foot until they were side by side. "What are *you* going to use for an excuse, Howie?" He laughed softly. "Well . . . shit!" He went quickly out of the bedroom, and downstairs.

From the narrow hall that ran through the center of the house he saw Laura in her white graduation dress on the front porch. She stood in front of the screen door with her back to him, her arms raised above her head, and for a moment, with rays of dusty sunlight slanting past her through the screen, she seemed suspended above the black strip of highway, silhouetted against the faded sky. Howard came up behind her. "You'll never do it."

Laura dropped her arms and turned. "Never do what?"

Howard closed his eyes and spread his arms. "Fly away, fly away home."

"That's real funny. I was drying my nails, for your information." She walked over to the edge of the porch and stood with one hand on the railing.

It was Margaret's wedding dress she had on, shortened and taken in at the waist. Where it was scalloped at the throat, delicate blue veins criss-crossed just beneath her skin which still glowed from the shower. Her hair was wheat-colored and reached her shoulders.

"I'll tell you something, if you won't take it too seriously." Howard came out on the porch and lit a cigarette. "What I mean to say, missy, is that there won't be an awful lot of people at this graduation looking the way you do."

Laura curtsied. "It's a pretty dress," she said. She touched her hair, then let her hand drop to the railing again. A red convertible sped past, its radio blasting electric guitar music. A soldier was behind the wheel. "Were you at all nervous?"

"When I graduated? Yeah, I guess. I guess most everyone is. I mean, it *is* a big day after all, after being in school for twelve years."

Laura took the cigarette from him. "It's not that; it's not this afternoon I'm nervous about. I guess it's just that this morning was the first time I really thought about how it would be to spend your whole life in Hargrett, saying hello to the same people and doing the things everybody else is doing—just growing old, Howie, without ever knowing anything else except maybe a trip somewhere once in a while."

Howard shrugged. "Hell, that's what everybody's nervous about, at least they are for a while. And especially everybody feels that way when they're getting out of high school. I know I did."

"Do you still feel that way?"

Howard boosted himself up on the railing. "What way? Oh . . . yeah, I do, I really do."

"Well are you ever going to leave then? I remember once you were thinking about trying to go to the university."

"Yeah, well I'm going to leave."

"When?"

Howard lit another cigarette and blew the smoke skyward. "You know something? I believe I've already covered this one time today, and the way I figure it, once for the day just ought to about fix it for a while. And besides, this is supposed to be the day everyone's bothering about *you,* not me."

Laura frowned and looked into the house. "It's different for me, for a girl. I just can't pick up and leave without any money and not knowing anybody outside of Hargrett, not anybody."

Howard flipped the cigarette into the yard. "Well, one thing with me is maybe I don't think I should leave *them.*" He nodded toward the house. "In case anything should happen."

"Oh Howie, what could happen if you weren't here that couldn't just as well happen if you were?"

"Lots of things. And besides, my salary from Kearney's helps them out a lot." He walked down to the far end of the porch, looking at the tractor in the side yard, then came back. "Anyway, what about *you,* little sister? Suppose for instance you should marry that sweet Burt Curtis? That'd sure be one way of getting out."

Laura blushed. "That's really funny, Howie; did you know that? Since you're so wonderful would you mind telling me what you've got against Burt?"

Howard put his hands up in front of him. "Who ever said I had anything against him? I like him. I do—old Burtis Curtis. *Are* you going to marry him?"

Laura smoothed her hair and twisted a strand around her finger. "Who says he's even asked me anything about that?"

"Well he will, he will. That's not the problem. The only problem is whether you want to marry him—him and the Burt Curtis Insurance Agency, the Burtis Curtis Insurance Service."

Laura turned to face her brother directly. "You really enjoy making fun of Burt, don't you? Well I'll tell you one thing, Mr. soda jerker, Burt's got a good chance of becoming a full partner in his cousin's business in Houston, and the only reason you make fun of him is because you're jealous, because Burt's only a few years older than you and he's making something of himself, not just sitting back and watching the world go by so he can make funny remarks at it. And if he asks me to marry him I just might do it, and when I get to Houston or some place I'll think about you back here making chocolate sodas. I just might marry Burt if he asks me, because maybe I *do* love him and because I'm not just talking about wanting to leave. I really want to, and you don't and never will!"

Howard drew a circle with his toe on the porch floor. "Well," he said after a while, "you about finished?" A grasshopper smacked against his side, and he craned his neck to see if it had left a spot on his white shirt.

"Yes," Laura said, not looking at him.

"Okay then, suppose just for something different . . ." He paused, then started again. "Did you ever by any chance think of the idea that I just might *not* be afraid of anything, that I might just have some plans of my own, and before I take out of Hargrett—I mean take out for *good,* little sister, not just leave for a while and then come slinking back with my tail between my legs—that I might want to make sure exactly what I'm going to do? You might think about that for a minute; I mean, you do that, because when I leave it's going to be for good and I'm going to be leaving to *do* something, not just for the sake of leaving."

Laura giggled and tossed her hair. "Whatcha gonna do, ol' Howie, head for Austin and run for governor?"

Howard nodded. "Speaking of funny remarks, that's about the funniest, cleverest thing I've had the privilege to hear in a long time."

"It's on the table," their mother called from the kitchen.

Laura touched Howard's sleeve. "We'd better go in."

He looked at her and put his hands in his pockets. "You go ahead; I'll be in in a minute." Laura hesitated. "No, it's all right," Howard said. "I was just thinking they might like to see you alone for a minute in that dress of yours. They haven't seen you in it yet, at least Papa hasn't. I'll be right in." He touched her lightly on the back of the neck.

Laura paused with her hand on the doorknob. "I'm just asking you not to spoil things, Howie. I know what you're thinking, and it's not true, and you don't have any right." She went into the house.

Howard leaned back against the screen door. A truck jammed with sheep went by, the animals' noses poking at air through the wire enclosure, their wool caked with red dirt. And far across the highway, out in the desert, dust clouds rose in a small wind that would never reach the porch. Even as Howard stood there watching, it died.

As he came into the kitchen, he could tell that only just then had his father looked away from Laura, and could tell from his father's expression that he was seeing his daughter in the white dress as a young woman. In his mother's eyes Howard saw the same realization, but saw too that while part of her thoughts were with her daughter, another part, further back behind her eyes, were of the old wedding dress.

But as they sat down, it was Shaylor who said, "You're wearing something to live up to today, Laura, so you'd better be sure you do us proud in that graduation." He reached over and squeezed her arm, then leaned back in his chair and looked across at Margaret. "You kids ought to have seen your mother the first time I saw her in that dress. I believe she was the prettiest bride in the state of Texas, coming down that aisle on her daddy's arm, and me waiting for her there, feeling kind of shaky—not from being nervous, but because me and Boyd had tied one on the night before." Margaret, Laura and Howie had begun to eat, but Shaylor only picked up his fork and toyed with his food.

"That was a long time ago, Jess," Margaret said. "They don't want to hear all about that again."

"Yeah, but it don't seem so long ago. Remember that suit I had on—the dark blue suit with the vest that I sent all the way to New Orleans for—standing there waiting for you, with Boyd holding the ring, and me with three hundred and fifty dollars in my pocket? That was a lot of money in those days and it took the price of one of my best breeders to get it there."

"You sold it just for the wedding?" Howard asked.

"Well, it was either the breeder or your mother. I had to make a choice."

"Don't think it was too easy a choice either," Margaret laughed.

"Some of the boys figured I was coming out a loser." Shaylor winked. "But I told 'em that as far as breeders go . . . well, never mind what I said; I forget anyway."

Across the table, Margaret stared at the wooden salad bowl; then, hearing her husband snicker, rose to take away the plates and said brightly, "I guess you'd *better* forget, Jesse Shaylor. Fine way to talk in front of your children, as if I was some prize heifer you got off the trading block." Shaylor laughed gratefully, not looking at her.

"What about the wedding?" Laura asked. Her eyes met Howard's as she got up to help her mother.

"You mean I never told you about that?"

"Oh Jess," Margaret said behind him, "they must have heard about it a million times."

Shaylor leaned forward and loosened his tie. "Three hundred and fifty dollars was a lot then. We rented the upstairs of Chet Coulter's place in Urando; remember, Maggie—with the piano player in the corner, and that fellow with the accordion and the ones we had in white coats serving champagne from San Antonio and bottles of beer and anything else you could want?" Margaret and Laura came back to the table. "There must have been two hundred people there at one time. And then later, toward evening, we barbecued a steer out in the back yard. You kids should have seen it!" Shaylor's voice was filled with wonder. "You should have seen it on that spit, turning slowly over that pretty fire that looked like it'd dropped right out of the sunset, the steer turning and getting golden brown and dripping juice onto the coals. It was a beautiful sight, that steer just hanging there against the sky, and for a while we all just sat and didn't even say a word, watching it cook and listening to it sizzle. Remember that, Maggie?"

Margaret was polishing a serving spoon with her apron. "It *was* beautiful."

"And after that, when it was time for us to go, I could have had the loan of a car if I'd wanted it—Charlie Wright's Packard. But I had something better planned, didn't I, Maggie? Tell 'em what it was."

"Oh Jess, they know already. They've heard it before." Margaret took a handkerchief from inside her blouse and dabbed her forehead. "Does everyone want coffee? There isn't much time."

"I'll get it," Howard said. "You just stay put."

"Mag?" Shaylor asked softly. "Ain't you going to tell them?"

"Well, it was a rig, a rig with two horses."

"That's what it was all right!" Shaylor slapped the table. "It sure was a rig with two of the prettiest white horses you ever saw. And there wasn't no one, no one at all, who knew I'd rented them a couple of days before from a fellow with a livery stable. And you know what I did the day before the wedding? I spent the whole day scrubbing down the two horses and grooming 'em and polishing the rig until its brass was bright as lightning and until . . . well anyway, just before it was time for us to go I said to everybody around, 'now you just wait here a minute and I'll be right back; I just got to step down the road and take care of something.' And then when I came back, you should have seen the faces; you should have seen them when I pulled right up smack in front of the fire with those two horses white as snow and that rig all shining and sparkling. You should have seen your mother's face."

"It sounds wonderful," Laura said.

"Yeah, and we drove it all the way to Elkinsville where we were catching the train for Galveston, but first we spun out around the ranch . . . well, it was only a three-room shack and twenty-five acres, but there were seventy head, Howie, seventy, and they looked pretty fine that night." Shaylor started to speak again, then sat back in his chair.

"Well, I guess we should be going," Laura said, looking into her coffee cup.

"Jess . . ." Margaret began.

Shaylor sat there, letting his gaze rest for a moment on each of them. "Well, of course that was a long time ago," he said, and slowly pushed himself up from the table.

Howard got up with him. He allowed himself to wonder how long his father would have to wait to die.

It is a new and different world you are entering. Yes, it is, a world in which you and I can travel across the country in a few hours, and across the globe in less time than it took our grandparents to reach the Oklahoma border. Men are in space, we all know that; hurtling at thousands of miles per hour around our world, heading for other worlds. You have been born into this new world and perhaps have even come to take it for granted. Grace Cowley pause to take a sip of water from a paper cup. Behind her, the purple-and-white curtain—school colors—moved austerely in the breeze from the giant air conditioners mounted in the wings of the brightly lighted stage. On her left was an American flag; on her right stood the state flag of Texas. Miss Cowley, tall and slender, was thirty-five and in her eleventh year as senior high school English teacher. After graduating from the university she had spent a year in London, and even now she retained the ghost of a British accent so that her words came over the amplifier in a soft staccato.

In the balcony, Burt Curtis was looking at the crease in his tan cord trousers. He had bought the suit last week in Houston while he had been shopping for Laura's graduation watch. The watch, had she been pleased with it? She seemed to be, but sometimes it was hard to tell what was really on her mind. And of course there was the confusion of standing around the schoolyard with her parents and Howie and all those other people milling around, and Laura waiting to join her class procession. What he'd wanted to say when he handed her the box was that this might be just a preview of another trip he might be making to the jewelry store pretty soon. He'd rehearsed that—

how he would just say it casually. But of course he hadn't been able to bring if off, not with the funny way Mr. and Mrs. Shaylor were looking at him when Laura unwrapped the package. Burt stole a look at his own gold pocket watch that had been left to him by his father. Seventeen years ago Bradley Curtis had driven a load of watermelons to Omaha; after two months he had sent his wife the watch and a fifteen-hundred-dollar money order from the sale of the truck, and had not been heard of since. Pauline Curtis had taken a job in Kibby's dress shop, stepped up her church attendance, and spoken of her husband to no one but Burt; and no one had spoken of him to her, though for a while, when some of Bradley's friends got drunk at the Lone Star, they'd sing a song that went:

Ol' Brad Curtis hopped in his truck
Headin' for Omaha to change his luck,
Whatever he was lookin' for he must've found there
'Cause we ain't seen him since, not a hide nor a hair.

And to her son, sitting on the edge of his bed after prayers, or walking home from church Sunday morning, Pauline would say, "We won't hate him for what he did to us, will we Burtie? Not a man we can hate, only a man we can feel sorry for; a man without substance and without purpose in life who's making his own purgatory for himself while you and I lead the lives of Christians and work for our goals the way the Lord meant for us to do." There were times when Burt was not altogether sure what those goals were, but there were never times when he doubted that the alternative to seeking them was a life of endless wandering, a life to be despised and pitied by everyone who came in contact with you, a life to be forgotten by your own family.

They're walking around under the sea, too—thousands of feet down in the fathomless depths, where no man has ever been before. All this is new! Man is exploring the heights and depths of his existence.

Howard, aware of Burt next to him, leaned forward and picked out Laura below, four rows from the front. Well then, what's it going to be, little sister? You really are going to marry him, aren't you. All right then, that's going to be the way you get out of here, away from your papa with his dreams of the past, and Momma with no dreams at all, and me with my soda jerk dreams. Get away from here with Burtie who's got real plans. So it has to be Burt because you couldn't do it all by yourself. You couldn't just get up some morning and say, "Well, I think maybe I've spent enough of my life in Hargrett and it's time I better be leaving." You couldn't do it, and not for the reasons you said; not because you're a girl, but because you know *they'll* never leave, not one fine morning, not ever. And maybe I won't either. And if you tried to do it on your own, it would be too much like running away, without ever knowing for sure what you were leaving. That's it, isn't it? You could go a thousand miles away, but how could you ever hope to get anywhere if you didn't even know what you were leaving? You can do it if you marry Burt, though, because all you'll have to say is "I'm with him; I'm traveling with him." There won't be any excuses needed then, little sister; you won't have to give an excuse to anyone in the world except maybe yourself.

But is it new after all? After all the missiles and the rockets, the automobiles and the machines, the supermarkets and the superhighways isn't it after all the same old world our forefathers faced? Some say that into this so-called new world one must bring new ideas, new concepts. That is true, I agree. But today, right now, I would hope that y'all . . . that you all sitting before me have not forgotten what I like to think of as the Old Values.

Laura folded her arms and moved further down in the seat, conscious of Miss Cowley's voice only as a background to her own thoughts, smelling musty velvet, tarnished band instruments, wax from the polished stage, all mingling in the sterile current of the air conditioners. How awful to have been so rude to Burt, practically throwing his present back in his face. She opened her eyes and stared at the enormous gilded head of a longhorn steer hanging above the stage, its horns extending over the orchestra pit. Had she acted that way because as soon as she'd seen the package she'd known it was a watch or a necklace instead of an engagement ring? Or was it because she had been afraid that Burt *was* going to give her the ring right there, right there standing in the school driveway with her parents and Howie watching or looking at the ground and shifting from one foot to the other, and maybe Mrs. McCloy or even Lou Tucker peeking over Burt's shoulder for a good look. And that would be it. Burt would say, "I figured as long as you're joining up with the grown-ups today, it'd be as good a time as any to ask you something that's been on my mind for a long time, and I guess you know what it is, Laurie."

But that *hadn't* been it, and what was it she was feeling now—disappointment that it hadn't happened, or leftover fear that it *could* have? No, not fear. Because she did love Burt, no matter what Howie wanted to believe, and Burt would care for her and make a good life for them. When he got around to asking her, she would say "yes" and believe "yes" and know she could wait a long time before someone came along who cared for her as much as Burt. And she would be waiting right here in Hargrett, at a desk in the First National Bank or behind a counter at Wilson's, waiting in her parents' house with the rusty, useless barbed-wire fence in back and the highway in front. Waiting.

I mean the old values of truth and responsibility, of honesty and faith, of love—values that have not changed. Despite the complexities of this modern world, these are the values that will bring us—each and every one of us—everything we will ever want or need.

Shaylor edged closer to Margaret. "That watch must have cost him seventy-five dollars. Did you see it?" Margaret put her hand over his. "So what do we do with this thirty-dollar thing we bought? She'll be expecting us to give her something."

"She's too excited to notice," Margaret whispered. "It'll be all right, Jess; we can take it back to Lyle's in the morning and exchange it for something else—a bracelet or a string of cultured pearls. She'd like that."

Shaylor drummed his fingers on the armrest. "Yeah, well tomorrow's Sunday, Meg, and when we're all sitting around at the drugstore she'll be wondering why we haven't given her anything."

Margaret sighed. "We'll just have to say that we ordered it special and it'll be here Monday."

"Well we'll see if she believes it." Shaylor looked around the dim auditorium, then leaned toward his wife again. "Did I tell you I'll be having to go out again tonight? And I'll probably have to stay out real late." Margaret smiled at Lucy Belknap who had turned to them from the row in front with a finger to her lips.

Missiles were built because there were men who believed in missiles, had faith in them. And you sitting before me today are our missiles. Today you are being launched into the future, and I ask you to remember that there are no shortcuts to your targets. There may be quicker ways to the Oklahoma border, to the far reaches of the world, but the old values are still the best means of traveling the road that now lies before you. So whether you journey to the far corners of the earth, or no farther than the corners of Main and Crescent, the old values of which I have spoken cannot but make your expedition a successful one.

There was a hush in the auditorium, then applause while Miss Cowley bowed to all corners. Then the school band played the alma mater, the national anthem and "The Eyes of Texas."

Howard and Burt waited by the curb as parents, relatives and graduates filed out the front door. Howard lit a cigarette. "Tell me, Burtie. How are your old values hanging?"

Burt laughed. "Pretty corny, wasn't it? Still, if you really think about it, you *do* have to have a few guideposts along the way, don't you think?"

Howard nodded. "At least a few."

"I remember when my mother used to say . . . I mean if *he'd* had some kind of principles to hold on to, he might not have taken off like he did."

"I suppose that's one way of looking at it."

Burt started to say something, then spotted Laura. "How you feeling about now, Laura?" he called in a voice louder than he had planned. "No more teacher's dirty looks, eh?"

Laura came up beside Howard. "I don't feel any different right now, not yet." Her father and mother joined them.

"Congratulations," said Shaylor. Margaret kissed her on the cheek, and the five of them stood without speaking for a moment. The courthouse bell struck three o'clock, and as if submerged under layers of afternoon heat, the metallic sound waves swam across the ground, lingering about the knees of the clusters of people talking and laughing in the schoolyard. Laura waved to someone.

"Well then," Howard said. "Are we all Kearney's-bound?"

"Kearney's?" Laura asked.

"Howard was thinking he might treat us all to sodas in honor of the occasion," Margaret said. "But if you have somewhere else to go, you run right along."

"It's just that I wish I'd known earlier." Laura hesitated. "Mary Jean Cameron kind of invited Burt and me and some other people over to her house."

"If I were you, I'd run along and have some fun," Shaylor said quickly. "I don't believe I much feel like one of those sodas anyway."

"Couldn't we do both?" Burt asked. "I think it would be nice, all sitting around Kearney's for a while."

"No, I say you get a move on." Shaylor took Margaret's arm. "I've got a lot of things to attend to anyway. We'll see you all a bit later." They started toward the truck, and then Shaylor stopped and turned. "We got a real nice present for you, by the way, Laura. It'll be . . ." He looked at Margaret.

"It'll be here by Monday," Margaret said. "We had to order

it special, and by all rights it certainly should be here Monday."

"Special? You didn't have to go to all that trouble, you didn't!" Laura took a step toward them. "Thank you, thank you both. I just can't hardly wait till Monday." Shaylor and Margaret got into the truck, and from the crowded schoolyard Laura and Burt and Howard waved as the truck started slowly down the street.

Burt patted his forehead with a handkerchief. "Why don't you come along for a while, Howie? As long as it's just the three of us. I won't feel like such an old man if you're along." Howard, hands on hips, was still watching the truck as it turned the corner of Crescent and headed across Tyler toward the highway.

"I'd really like that, but I better be getting over to the store." He put his hands on Laura's shoulders. "You both have one for me, hear? And you, Burtie, be careful this child doesn't get drunk."

"You come too," Laura said quickly.

Howard backed away. "I would, I would in a minute if it weren't for old man Kearney."

"You could come if you really wanted to, if you didn't have to stand around all the time pretending you know something that nobody else does, pretending you know what's going on inside everybody's head." She walked away and got into Burt's Rambler.

Burt looked at Howard. "What's that all about? All you said is you have to get to work."

"Don't worry about it, she's just nervous today. I'll see you all later." Howard watched them drive off, then started toward the store. As he walked along the sidewalk, he undid his necktie, mopped his face with it and stuffed it into his jacket pocket. The schoolyard had emptied. Howard cut through the Texaco station to Main Street, thinking of his father's face as he had gotten into the truck; his face for an instant had held not only despair, but the hardening resolution that despair could not be allowed to have its way much longer. We're beginning to know what you want, aren't we, Papa, beginning to know why you're so anxious to get me away from here, away from you. And it's not really that you want me to be another Burt, is it, or to make a big name, but just to get something going for myself so you can forget about me and get back to you, get back to that thing that's been itching at you and that I just saw. If only I was accounted for, you could think about settling your own little account. He broke off his thoughts, aware that a car was cruising along beside him.

It was a 1952 Hudson sedan with a black body and a mustard roof. The hubcaps had been painted black too, and along the side windows were borders of black fringe balls. A lowered venetian blind hung in the rear window. The car edged to the curb and stopped. Inside was Crow Turner.

"How you doing, Crow?" Howard said, coming over to the car. Seeing Crow's disappointed frown, he realized he had said the wrong thing. "What I mean," he added quickly, "is that it's a nice day, isn't it?"

Crow's face lit up instantly. "It's a nice day to get laid!" he whinnied. He killed the engine and slid over to the passenger side.

You couldn't tell how old Crow was, not only because his face was round and cherubic, but because his skin and wispy hair and eyebrows were all the same color—dusty tan—as if someone had not yet brushed in the shadows and tints that would give a clue to his age. No one had ever taken the time to figure out just how long he had been around Hargrett, or where he lived, where he came from, how he spent his time. Crow would disappear for two or three weeks or even months at a time, and then you'd catch a glimpse of the Hudson streaking along the highway, or come upon it parked near the railroad tracks, its hood and trunk agape, like a giant two-headed slug. Crow, surrounded by piles of tools and spare parts and tires and oily rags, would be hunched next to the body—probing, examining, petting.

Crow leaned against the window frame and rested his chin on his arms. "I'd like to ask you when is the last time *you* got laid, Howie, let's say inside the period of the last two weeks. In that particular period, how many times you been laid?"

Howard scratched his head. "I don't honestly believe I can tabulate it right here on the spot, Crow. I mean it would take some thinking."

Crow looked at him for a moment through narrowed eyes, then hugged his arms and began to rock back and forth. "You're lyin'! You're lyin'!" he shrieked. "I'll bet if you said even *one* damn time it wouldn't be true!"

Howard shrugged. "Where do you think I'm coming from now, as a matter of fact?"

Crow stopped rocking and puckered his lower lip thoughtfully. "What're you trying to say?"

"I'm not trying to say anything. I just asked you a question."

"Oh no you don't!" Crow cackled suddenly. "Oh no! I saw you coming out of that schoolyard from the graduation, so I *know* where you been, and you ain't coming from no getting laid, so don't you try to fool me, Howie Shaylor. I can tell when a man's been laid or not, and I just know you didn't get laid at no graduation."

"Lots of rooms in that schoolhouse, Crow." Howard stroked his chin and gazed over the roof of the car.

Crow pounded on the window frame with both fists. "I don't want to hear any more of that, Howie! Now you listen to me. I'm telling you *I* get laid any day I feel like it, and that's the truth." He stuck his head out the window and looked up and down the street. "Listen, Howie, I been *doing* some things since the last time I saw you, and that's not just talk either. Don't ask me to tell you what it is 'cause I can't, but I'll tell you I been traveling with somebody that . . ." Crow stopped, but before he did, something in his voice made Howard look at him closely.

"What is it, Crow? What are you trying to say?"

"Nothing. But this person wouldn't team up with anybody if

he didn't think they could deliver the goods. You see, him and me are good pals. I mean, we see things the same way." On the inside of Crow's right forearm was a purple tattoo that said DEATH BEFORE DISHONOR. "You just don't know, Howie, you just don't have any idea in the world." He slid over behind the steering wheel again. "Look, I gotta go now. Maybe I'll see you later." He started the engine, gunned the Hudson into a screeching U-turn, and headed out toward the highway in a cloud of blue exhaust. Howard stood there a moment, then started walking to the drugstore again.

That evening the wind that had wandered about the desert all day came to town. It ruffled the banners of Mason Blake's used-car lot, and rattled the Texaco sign and teased the clacker of the courthouse bell, filling the square with gentle intermittent ringing.

Laura sat on the courthouse lawn next to Burt, feeling the wind on her neck and remembering that when she had been six or seven, still living at the old ranch, a trucker had given her a young cherry tree that her father had planted next to the house. They had bought silver bells at the five-and-ten-cent store to keep the birds away, and Howard had tied them to the branches. At night in bed she would hear the wind blowing the bells in the cherry tree and would imagine that they were the bells of some faraway town through whose streets she walked, walking so independently that people could not help but turn and watch her and wish to touch her hair. They would be surprised at her grown-up answers to their questions and would know she was a special girl. They would like it when she wore her golden hair in one long braid, and they would like it when it fell free about her shoulders and caught the sunlight. The next summer they had moved away; but even before that the tree had died, and now she wondered if it was still standing, if the bells, now rusty and corroded on the dead branches, still rang in the night winds.

She turned to Burt. "Where will we live?"

"Don't you worry about that," he chuckled. "We'll get an apartment at first—a nice one. And then after a while, after I've gotten established, there's no reason we shouldn't start looking for a house. The way I figure it, there's no point in keeping on paying rent for an apartment when you could just as well be paying off a mortgage. Besides, we might be thinking about a family before long." He stretched his arms. "Don't you worry, Laurie, we're going to have nice places to live in."

Laura could see into the windows of Kearney's across the square and see Howard wiping off the soda fountain. "Burt, can you . . . I mean, can you handle things?"

"What do you mean, Laurie?"

She lay back on the grass. The stars of the Texas sky seemed almost close enough to touch. "I guess I was talking about me, not you. Sometimes, *most* of the time, it's as if I can feel what everyone else is doing. I can feel my father living in the past, and Momma just hanging on with him, taking care of him as if he was still a little boy. And I can feel you too, your plans and your strength. But with me, and maybe with Howie too, there isn't anything to feel except just kind of a waiting for somebody to tell us what to do. Only no one's going to tell us, are they?"

Burt leaned forward and hugged his knees. An automobile was moving slowly along one side of the square, its headlights reflecting in store windows. "Maybe you're just rushing things a little. I guess the way I figure it is, it doesn't make a lot of difference what you do as long as you stick to it. I mean, my father ran away; he just ran away from everything, and I'm not going to do that. I'm going to stick to my plans. I'm going to have my own business in a few years, Laurie." He lay down on his stomach, leaning on one elbow so that his face was above hers. "I guess it isn't easy for anyone. I mean, my father left me wanting to make something out of myself; but your mother and dad are still around, and maybe you feel if you leave Hargrett you'll be deserting *them.* But you wouldn't be, Laurie; they want you to lead your own life."

Laura sat up again. "I'm *going* to go with you, Burt. We're not even *like* a family. We watch each other, all of us, even Momma. No, it's not even like that; it's as if all four of us live inside the same skin and anything that happens to one happens to the rest. It's not just that I can feel Momma and Papa; I've gone through their lives with them, and they're still waiting to go through mine. It's as if they're afraid of my future and I'm afraid of their past."

Burt stood up and put his hands in his pockets. "I guess it's pretty important for you to leave Hargrett, any way you can."

Now Laura got up quickly. "I didn't mean it that way, the way it sounded."

He put his hands on her shoulders. "I know. I didn't mean it either. I love you, Laurie; you know that. We're going to have a good life."

She leaned against him. "We will. I know we will. And all these things—just don't pay any attention to them. It'll only be at first that you'll have to be strong enough for me too. After that, when we get away, I'll be all right, you'll see. Because I love you too, I do." Over Burt's shoulder, just before he kissed her, she saw Howard pull down the shade in the drugstore window.

Howard had seen them too. He had seen Burt's Rambler parked across the square and had picked out the white dress on the courthouse lawn. After he had pulled the shade, he waited with his back to the door until he heard the motor start and the Rambler drive off. Then he went over to the fountain and stood twirling one of the circular seat tops.

Someone knocked on the glass door. "We're closed!" Howard called without turning. There was another knock. He walked over to the door. The green shade reached about three-quarters of the way down. Below it, crouched on the step, her face raised to him, was Grace Cowley. "I'm sorry to trouble you, Howard. I just wanted to pick up some aspirin if you're still open. For my mother." Howard squatted so their faces were inches apart. Miss Cowley's skirt had hiked up over her knees, and the corsage given her by the graduating class was being crushed at her waist. "Mother's all out of aspirin, and she's just getting over a cold." Howard remained squatting for a moment, then stood and unlocked the door. "I forgot you closed this early," Miss Cowley said as he latched the door behind her. "I expect I'm holding you from an engagement." Howard smiled and went behind the drug counter.

"Bottle of aspirin all you need, Miss Cowley?"

"What's that, Howard? Yes, that's all . . . just getting over a cold." Her voice trailed, and Howard leaned his elbows on the glass counter.

"That was a nice speech you gave at the graduation."

Miss Cowley came to a halt in front of the sunglasses tree. Pinned above her bosom on her white blouse was a purple-and-white "Go Steers Go!" button. "I said I thought you gave a fine speech."

She stood there a moment longer, then came over to the counter. "Yes, but I expect you're poking fun at me, aren't you?"

Howard felt in his pockets for his cigarettes. "No, I wasn't doing that, I wasn't making fun. Well, maybe I was, but not at you *personally*. I mean, it *was* a good speech. It was a good thing for someone to say at a graduation." He blew a stream of smoke across the counter, and Miss Cowley sidestepped it.

"It's the same speech I gave last year," she said softly.

"I know. It's the same one you gave three years ago when I graduated. Do you think you'd like a quick cup of coffee, Miss Cowley? I've got some left in the pot."

"Coffee?" Miss Cowley smiled down at the counter. "No, perhaps not. It *is* getting late, and you'll be wanting to close, and Mother's waiting for the aspirin. But thank you, Howard, I ordinarily would enjoy it."

Howard put the bottle in a bag. "That's all you needed then?"

"Yes, that's all. Just the aspirin." She searched in her purse for money. "Three years ago I gave it? I *did?* Oh my! Perhaps I gave it the year before that too. And the year before *that.*" She laid a dollar on the counter and stood with her lips pressed together. "But it's not altogether my fault, you see. Because every year Mr. Morris will say at a faculty meeting, 'Got your speech all ready, Miss Cowley? Got to start these young people off with a bang on the road of life.' " Howard rang up her change. "And then I never know what to say, Howard. I can never think of anything to say at the moment. I expect all the others have come to think of it as a kind of tradition by now—a comic tradition probably—Miss Cowley and her graduation speech. But no one *else* ever volunteers, Howard, and I expect they're just as happy to let me do it every year, don't you imagine?" She put her hand over the coins on the counter. "Was it *exactly* the same?"

Before Howard could answer, there was another knock at the door. Beneath the shade was a pair of blue-denim legs.

"You in there, Howie?"

"What do you need, Crow?"

"That you, Howie? It's me, Crow."

"What do you want, Crow?"

"Howie? Look, I figured on taking a spin over to Beeville for a couple of beers or something. How soon you going to be finished up?"

Howard looked at Miss Cowley's hand. "Can't make it, hoss; I'm taking inventory and I've got to stay here awhile!"

There was a pause, then Crow shouted, "You want a drink right now?" A whisky bottle, held by its neck, appeared below the shade and was rapped against the glass. Grace Cowley busied herself with the clasp of her handbag.

"Yeah, I'd like it just fine, but I just fixed myself a soda so maybe I better not." The legs disappeared.

"I just didn't feel like it," Howard explained to Miss Cowley, who hadn't moved. "I guess there are a lot of times when I figure there's more to life than just going out for beers."

"I would say that's something for which to be glad, Howard. It seems that so many young people, at least many of the ones with whom I've come in contact, seem rather frivolous. Of course I realize that that may be because I'm no longer young."

"You're still young," Howard said quickly. "I consider you to be still young."

"Oh," Miss Cowley said. "Well, I don't *feel* old, Howard. I have a very rich life, teaching. And I didn't mean to make it sound as if *all* my students are frivolous. I've had some very worthwhile pupils in my classes, some that have gone on to do important things."

Howard went over to the opposite side of the store and turned off the lights over the soda fountain. "I enjoyed having you in school, Miss Cowley."

"I could tell that *you* were the serious type too, Howard. In fact, I've often wondered why . . ." Howard made a noise. "What was that, Howard? What did you say?"

"Nothing, Miss Cowley. I'll walk you home." He held the door open and waited for her, then locked it behind them, leaving the orange night light burning in the glass cigar case.

The air had become cool, and the moon had risen above the bell tower of the courthouse. As they turned left on Main Street, Howard put his hand lightly on Miss Cowley's elbow.

Her living room smelled of apples and wallpaper. Except for the large blue-velvet couch along one wall and a squat maple bookcase, all the furniture stood on thin legs—the small piano in one corner, the desk in another, the two high-backed chairs diagonally facing the couch, the round-topped, ivory-inlaid mahogany table between them, and next to the couch, the white marble-topped side table upon which stood a tall metal replica of the Tower of London.

Miss Cowley went out of the room, and Howard sat down in one of the chairs, crossed his legs, uncrossed them, got up, and sat down on the couch. The cushion collapsed beneath him and he sank in, his feet leaving the floor. He could make his heels touch the oriental rug only if he stretched his legs and pressed them down hard against the cushion. Otherwise, they hovered two inches above the rug, his body at a slight tilt.

Miss Cowley returned. With a push of his elbows against the back cushion and a pump of his legs, Howard managed to get to his feet.

"Do sit down, Howard," Miss Cowley said, sitting in one of the diagonal chairs. "Would you like an apple?" She passed him the bowl from the mahogany table.

"No, maybe not; no thank you, Miss Cowley. I *am* a little thirsty though, to tell the truth, if it wouldn't be a lot of trouble."

"It isn't any trouble at all, Howard; it's my pleasure." She got up and left the room again, and Howard readjusted himself on the couch.

"Will orange juice be all right?" Miss Cowley called from the kitchen. "There doesn't seem to be any soda."

"Orange juice is fine!"

"What did you say? Did you want something?"

"What's that?" Howard called back. "No, I didn't say anything. Just the orange juice is fine!"

"A glass of water?" Miss Cowley shouted. "I'll be right in. Would you rather have orange juice?" Howard felt for his cigarettes.

Miss Cowley passed by in the hall, and a few moments later went by from the opposite direction; then she came into the living room with two glasses of orange juice which she set down on the mahogany table. Howard braced himself for the journey to his feet, but Miss Cowley sat down quickly in one of the diagonal chairs. She smoothed her skirt. "That was Mother. That's who I was talking to."

And then neither of them spoke.

"I suppose," Miss Cowley said, after both were holding their glasses, "that you might wonder occasionally why a person like me remains in Hargrett."

"Well to tell the truth, I do; I sure do occasionally wonder that."

She sipped her juice. "Yes. Well, of course some of it's because of Mother. She's deaf, almost completely deaf. So it would be difficult for her to move to some place such as London or

New York City if I should happen to decide to move to one of those places."

Howard nodded. "I guess it *would* be hard for a deaf person to just pull up roots."

"It wouldn't be easy for one to adjust to a totally new environment."

"Difficult," Howard said.

Miss Cowley got up and stood behind her chair. "And then of course since Daddy's been gone I'm all she has."

"Yeah," Howard said, "that's right too. How long is it now?"

"That he's been gone? Well, since I was . . . it's going on sixteen years now, although I often find it hard to believe it's that long." She put her hands on the back of the chair and stared at the floor.

"Oklahoma City?" Howard asked after a while.

"Kansas City. When we last heard from him. He sends checks."

"Well, that helps." Howard shielded his cigarette and flicked an ash between the couch cushions.

"Yes," Miss Cowley said vaguely, coming over to sit next to him, "but I believe I know what you're thinking, Howard. You're wondering what would get into a man to just up and leave his family like that. Well, all I can say is that I just don't know." She cocked her head. "Mother, is that you? Do you need anything?" She turned back to Howard. "It's an odd natural phenomenon; the deafer Mother has become over the years, the more acute *my* sense of hearing has become. I don't expect you even heard anything from her room just now. I can hear her though—practically the slightest sound, no matter what part of the house I'm in."

On the table there was a crystal plate that could have been either an ashtray or a candy dish. Howard jabbed his cigarette butt into the center of it.

"I've thought about it quite frequently of course," Miss Cowley continued. "I mean, it would naturally be a subject that would come to mind over the years, him being my father. And I suppose what I feel is that he just didn't have enough confidence to know where he properly belonged. Now I admit that seems to contradict itself." She shifted on the couch so she faced Howard directly. "I believe that in the bottom drawer of that side table with the replica of the Tower of London on it, Howard, there is a bottle of gin." They were silent while he found it, poured an inch of gin into each orange juice glass, put the bottle on the mahogany table, then picked it up again and put it on the floor. "But what I mean is that there have been many times I've thought that I myself might be . . . well, better suited to a life elsewhere—in New York City perhaps, or London. I mean, my instincts might be more in sympathy with the kind of people that one probably won't find here in Hargrett and that probably won't ever come here." Miss Cowley looked into the hall a moment, then took another swallow of her drink. "But I have roots here; that's important, you know." She touched Howard's wrist. "I mean, even if I personally might occasionally wonder if I'd be more adapted to a place elsewhere, I feel that my life here, my career in teaching, gives me a very full life; in fact, perhaps an even fuller life than I would find elsewhere." She leaned toward him, her eyes on his face. "Can you understand that, Howard? Do you see this point I'm making?"

Her lips were parted slightly, and Howard could see a trace of lipstick on her teeth. "Well, I guess what you're saying is that you kind of belong here in Hargrett."

Her hand went to her throat. *"Belong* here, Howard? *Belong* here?" Her hand dropped to the neck of the gin bottle.

"Well, not that you *belong,"* Howard said quickly, "or that you're like everyone else in Hargrett. I mean, everybody can see that you're not." Miss Cowley leaned back. Howard had put his arm along the back of the couch, and now her collar came in contact with his thumb.

"I'm not *better* than anyone else; I wouldn't want you to think that. You see, Howard, those of us who can see a world elsewhere are in a sense exactly the ones who should stay here so that perhaps we can bring some of that world to the people who aren't aware of it. You see, that's what's so rewarding about my career in teaching; I can translate this world to others."

Howard nodded. "I believe I understand what you're saying, Miss Cowley. Nobody really has to go anyplace as long as they know there's some other place to go, and the only ones who should go are the ones who don't know about any other places. Is that it, Miss Cowley?"

Miss Cowley sighed. "I can't remember when I've enjoyed communicating so much with someone, Howard; I can't help but feel a certain, what one could only call, bond between us. Does that sound silly?"

"Well, if you want to know the truth, I was thinking exactly that about a second before you said it."

"I'm pleased," Miss Cowley said. A fringe of her hair was between Howard's thumb and forefinger. "Occasionally I can't help wondering, Howard, what keeps you here in Hargrett."

Howard opened his mouth to speak, but then, from the back of the house, there came a thump followed by a crash and the tinkle of breaking glass. Miss Cowley stood up. "It's all right. Mother's fallen out of bed is all."

Howard followed her into the hall, then into a darkened room that smelled faintly of mouthwash and sour bed clothes. In the dim yellow glow from the hall light he could make out Miss Cowley's mother, covered and lying on what looked like a platform in the middle of the room. "It's another mattress," Miss Cowley said, "on a box spring. Mother falls out of bed practically every night, so I just put another mattress over the area she usually hits. Only, I forgot to move the lamp tonight. She must have hit it with an arm on the way down." Miss Cowley sighed. "You'll notice, though, that it didn't wake her; she didn't hear a thing. See, the sheet comes right with her; it hardly even gets wrinkled."

Howard looked. The jackknife shape beneath the sheet was capped by a cluster of metal curlers that glinted back at him. "Yeah," he said. "Do we leave her here?"

Miss Cowley was standing behind him. "Well, you see, we can't; you see, Mother wakes up just before dawn every morning to make a trip. At least it usually seems to be around that time. If she wakes up in a strange place, it could be difficult for her to adjust; that is, at her age."

Miss Cowley's mother was beginning to snore gently. Howard stepped back a pace from her. "Yeah, but it can't be *too* strange; I mean, if she ends up here every night."

"Oh, well you see, she doesn't really end up there, Howard. When she wakes up to make her trip she's always back in bed."

"And you're on the mattress."

"It's very comfortable. It's firm."

Howard nodded. "Shall I get her feet?"

"No, no," Miss Cowley said quickly. "I do this every night, really; I don't even think about it any more. She hardly weighs a thing."

"I'll get her feet."

Miss Cowley went around to the other side of the mattress. "The easiest way, I believe, is to kind of wrap her in the sheet and then each lift an end. Like a sling."

Howard tucked the sheet around her legs while Miss Cowley attended to the shoulders. "On three, Miss Cowley?"

"She hardly weighs a thing, Howard."

Wrapped, Miss Cowley's sleeping mother was lifted and deposited on the bed.

Howard watched while Miss Cowley smoothed the sheet. "Now let's see, if she falls again she falls on you, is that it?"

"Once a night is all," Miss Cowley said, fluffing the pillow, "about an hour after she goes to sleep. I slide my mattress down to the foot of the bed so she won't trip over it when she gets up." While she finished smoothing the bed, Howard moved the mattress. "There, all finished!" She leaned against the bedpost. "Howard, I just want to thank you for your help." She looked at him for a moment, then smiled and smoothed her hair back from her forehead. "And I don't mind if . . . well, if you think it's all pretty funny. I mean, it is; it is silly. But all of us do have habits that seem silly to others, don't you think? Don't you think we just take them for granted until we might have an occasion to see them through someone else's eyes? I mean, I wouldn't even mind if you should want to tell someone about it. That is, I could see how it might be an amusing story, the mattress on the floor and everything."

Howard started to say something, but he did not finish. Instead, he reached across the mattress and removed the "Go Steers Go!" pin and put it in his pocket.

And then Miss Cowley might have stumbled. Howard caught her and held her, his hands on her waist, her hair against his cheek, and felt, soon, dampness on his cheek and her legs and body against him so tightly that it was hard to breathe. Then their knees were pressing into the mattress.

"I'm not going to tell anyone, Miss Cowley. I'm not going to tell anyone."

Out on the highway the truck sped south, its headlights cutting through the darkness. The truck would do sixty; it wouldn't do sixty-five, and when Shaylor forgot and pushed it too hard the transmission would shriek, the hood and sideboards would rattle, and the whole truck would buck and shudder. He would have to hang onto the steering wheel and ride it out, feeling the vibrations from his wrist to shoulder, and only then would he let up on the accelerator. But even when he forgot, the right-hand wheels never got closer than a foot to the road shoulder; and even with his shirt soaked from the effort of staying in control, his eyes never left the macadam.

Out there, you are always in the dead center of the night. The highway races under you, whistling the wind past the sides of your car, carrying back with it towering black telegraph poles strung out along the far side of the gravel shoulder. Along the edge of the road, your headlights will pick out the thick curl of a sliced tire, a rusted can, the sudden spark of animal eyes. But mostly there is the road, a grainy, bejeweled belt. And the harder you press down on your gas pedal, the louder the wind whistles around you and the faster the belt races back under you. So you remain in the center of the night.

Out there, somebody could be in trouble. A generator fails or a fuel pump cuts out, and you sit by the road, wasting your battery on radio voices lost in static, taking what comfort you can from your dashboard lights. Once, twice an hour a giant aluminum trailer truck might come along, or a sedan with one headlight out, driving for the border, but they won't stop. They'll race by, buffeting you with a slap of air, and you'll sit there until morning, in the middle of the night.

And that was why he was cruising down the highway; for no other reason than that some poor fellow might be the victim of a broken-down car, with no one about to stop for him. If you thought about it, it was really part of his job. And Boyd had agreed. That is, he hadn't said anything when Shaylor had told him the idea, nor had Margaret. He'd started his patrol with one or two nights a week, but then, you could never tell when somebody might be stranded out there. In the past two weeks he had not missed a night, although, as yet, he had not come upon a stranded motorist.

He had driven eighty miles north to Belgian Corners, cut west on a farm road that skirted a field of oil rigs, picked up 37-A, and now was back on 37, two miles from the house. It was three o'clock in the morning. Not a bad thing to be doing—to want to help somebody; not done with the wild idea of gaining escape, to point the truck toward the Oklahoma border and to keep going, to run away from Hargrett toward a memory of himself. No, what he felt was a loss, a loss of time, so that the present merged into the past, and the hum of the engine brought a kind of peace and was an end in itself. There was nothing to be ashamed of. Whatever he'd had, he'd gotten by himself. And when he lost it . . . There was someone walking along the edge of the road.

Shaylor slowed the truck as the headlights focused in on the back of the walking figure and outlined his shadow in front of him; but it was not until he had driven two or three hundred feet past him that Shaylor braked hard, pulled over onto the gravel, and waited.

Howard came up beside the cab. "Didn't know if you'd recognize me, the way you were whipping along. You want me to drive?" Shaylor slid over to the passenger side while Howard got in behind the wheel. "The brakes okay?"

"They're still a little soft. I'll take a look at them tomorrow."

"I'll look at them." Howard edged the truck onto the blacktop. "Find anyone tonight?"

Shaylor rubbed the callouses of his palms. "Where you been, Howie? Where you coming from?"

"Coming from? Just a date. No place special. I guess it must be pretty late."

"Anyone I know?"

"Who? Oh, no, just someone who came into the store, and then we just went out and had a couple of drinks with some people."

Shaylor rolled down his window and rested his arm on the door. "Yeah, I guess one thing about that drugstore is it's pretty good for your social life." Howard didn't answer. "I mean, a lot of people coming in all the time that you can chew the fat with, just kind of stand around and make dates for drinking beer."

"Look, do we have to start up again right now? It's late, and I'm tired, and all I want to do is go to bed."

Shaylor turned away from the window. "Now you wait a minute! You don't tell me what to do! I'm your father; don't you try to shut me up. It's just too bad if you're tired."

"I wasn't trying to shut you up," Howard said carefully. "I just figured that it's late and we both had a long day and we're not going to settle anything by arguing." They passed Boyd's service station.

"Long day?" Shaylor laughed sharply. "What do you know about a long day?"

Without answering, Howard jammed his foot down on the brake, hard enough so that Shaylor had to brace himself against the dashboard. He pulled over onto the gravel and stopped. "I think I'm just going to walk; I'm going to walk the rest of the way if it's all right with you!" Howard started to get out, then paused with his hand on the door. "Look, you don't even know what we're talking about, what we're really talking about. Or maybe you do. Can't you understand it's not going to work—this trying to push me into something? Christ, Papa! I don't even know where *my* life begins and yours ends." Shaylor reached out a hand as if to grab him, but Howard got the door open, jumped down from the cab, and slammed the door behind him.

He began running down the center of the highway back toward town. A layer of mist hung over Ansino Creek. He looked back over his shoulder. The truck had not moved. As he ran the sweet green smell of the stagnant creek filled his lungs, and for a dizzying instant he stumbled and nearly fell. When his aching legs slowed him to a walk, he looked back again. He was on the other side of the bridge now, and through the mist from the creek he saw the red taillights growing smaller. He stood there in the middle of the highway, breathing hard, and watched until finally the lights were gone. There were crickets singing near the creek, and the wind that blew cool on his forehead and neck blew sagebrush across the road. Slowly, he began walking after the disappeared truck; then, after a few steps, he stopped again, waited, and turned back toward town. He thought of Miss Cowley asleep at the foot of her mother's bed and smiled. If he went back there, he'd arrive just in time to meet her mother in the middle of her trip. He was only about a quarter of a mile from Boyd's station, though. He could sleep there.

Then, behind him, he heard the sound of a motor. It would be the truck. He walked faster. "Don't do it," he whispered. "Just don't bother because there isn't any point to it, and it won't make any difference whatever we say."

But it was not the truck; it was a car which shot by him, then, a hundred yards past, squealed to a stop so sharply that its back end skidded around and the car came to rest straddling the highway. It was Crow's car. "That you, Howie?" Crow called out. "What's it you think you're doing out here?"

Howard waited until he was alongside the car before answering. "Just coming from getting laid again is all."

Crow spat out the window. "Well you want a ride some place?" Howard nodded, walked around the car, and got in. "You want a drink?" Crow asked after a while. He handed Howard a pint bottle. Howard took several swallows. It was gin. "Where you going to, Howie?"

"No place special. What about you?" He handed the bottle back.

"Me? Well I already *been* to Beeville, if that's what you mean." He tapped his fingers on the steering wheel. "So now I'm just going no place special. You want me to drop you off some place? I mean, I got to get back pretty soon. I had to get some things, and I'll be heading for where we're staying."

Howard took the bottle from him. "I think maybe there's a car coming. At least I can see some lights down the road." Crow shifted into reverse and shot backward to the shoulder, then gunned forward, the tires spitting gravel. A minute later they passed Boyd's garage, which was dark except for the yellow night light in the office. Howard closed his eyes. "Any objections to me coming along?"

"Objections? No, I ain't got any objections." Crow reached over for the bottle, finished it and tossed it out the window. The car picked up speed. "Why should I have any objections? Except that . . ."

"I know," Howard said without opening his eyes. "That other guy might not like you bringing a friend along. Well, that's all right, Crow. I understand."

"Shit!" Crow slapped the steering wheel. "What do you think it is? Him and me are *partners.* I told you that before. He ain't no *boss,* if that's what you're trying to say. Nobody's telling me anything about what I can't do."

Howard opened his eyes. "No, it's okay, Crow, I just figured, since we were buddies, it might be kind of nice to travel around a little together."

"We *will!*" Crow screeched. "We will! We're good buddies, Howie." He put his hand on Howard's knee. "Don't you worry,

Howie; ain't nobody pushes me around. I mean, it's my car, and that should count for something."

Howard patted Crow's hand. "It sure *does* count; it counts for a whole lot that nobody pushes you around." He belched. "Nobody pushes me around either."

Crow put his other hand over Howard's. "There ain't nobody ever going to say nobody ever pushes us around."

"NOBODY!" Howard shouted as the car veered across the highway, rode along the shoulder for fifty yards, and, before Crow grabbed the wheel, slid off the shoulder into a sand ditch and stalled. They sat there for two or three minutes.

"Shit! You okay, Howie?"

"Right. You?"

Crow switched off the ignition. "Well, maybe I'll get out and push."

Howard scratched his nose. "No, you stay here, buddy. *I'll* push. You gun it. You want a cigarette?"

"Yessir, I sure do." A truck was approaching. Beneath a border of red and green lights, its headlights caught particles of dust from the Hudson's trip into the ditch. It was a trailer truck. As it roared past, it gave a long blast on its air horn. "Altogether," Crow said after a minute, "I mean, starting with the first real time, how many times would you say you actually been laid?"

Howard put his hands behind his head. "Well the truth is, I've tried to figure that out myself, but you know, you just can't do it, Crow; you just can't keep track after a while."

Crow took a drag on his cigarette and let the smoke out in a sigh. "Yeah. Maybe you ought to try pushing us out while I gun it."

When the car was free they started off again. Howard watched the broken white line that split the blacktop. He tapped his tongue against the roof of his mouth in rhythm with the lines, then began to click his teeth.

"The only thing I was wondering," Crow said, "is what kind of method you use. I mean, I don't have a lot of trouble myself, if you want to know the truth, but I was wondering . . . well, let's say you see this little girl, maybe in a café or a bar, and you believe you'd like to screw her." He cleared his throat. "What would you do?"

Howard looked over at him for a second, then leaned back in the seat. "Well, hoss, I guess it would depend on what she looked like. There're a lot of different kinds of girls, and you just can't treat them all the same." The car picked up speed.

"Let's just say she looked like *anything*. You're sitting in this barroom and you see this little girl and you go over. I mean, *do* you go over, Howie, or do you maybe wait until she gives you some kind of sign?"

"It's hard to tell."

"Yeah. Well then, you go over and maybe you say something like, 'it's a hot day.' "

"Unless it isn't. If it was in a barroom, it might be night."

"Shit! Will you listen to me? You're there talking to her about something, and then do you get the conversation around to how you been looking for a little girl like her for a long time, and the minute you saw her you knew you could really go for her? Or do you just go on talking about anything that comes into your head, and maybe after a while put a hand on her ass?"

Howard rubbed his eyes. "It's really hard to tell, Crow, I guess what you have to do is play it by ear. What do you think *you'd* do?"

Crow sighed. "Hell, I was asking *you*. Anyway, like I was saying before, I don't have trouble that way."

Now they were driving through a cotton fog that hung low just over the blacktop. The Hudson raced through it at seventy-five miles an hour, the headlights knifing out wispy shapes an instant before they blew apart against the hood. Crow turned on the wipers, and with the steady rhythm to pace his thoughts, Howard tried to picture the scene when his father returned home.

Would he wake up his mother? No, he would wait until the

morning when she was making breakfast, with her back to him, unable to see his face. And his voice—would it be sarcastic? Relieved? Sad? He would look at the floor and run one finger along the edge of the kitchen table the way he always did when he was uncertain of his words or their impact. But what would he be feeling? Howard couldn't know. He could focus in on him, set the stage, pose him, but he'd still be on the outside and no better for having isolated him in his thoughts. And even if he did come up with an answer—a voice, the idea of an emotion—it would only be his idea of his father's mind, only an imitation. It would never change; there would always be the pain of trying to get through, and for what—to find the part of the deadness in his father's life that he was to replace or make up for? Should he have waited then, waited for the possibility of one moment when they might reveal themselves to each other? There had been that unguarded moment in the schoolyard, but his father had not been aware of it. And there was in Howard's mind the image of his father's hand outstretched in the truck, the hand that both reached out for him and pushed him away.

And his mother, who held back from both husband and son, who was so careful not to take sides, not to acknowledge the existence of sides: how would she react? Only one way, of course, only as the comforter. "It's all right, Jess; it's just something he had to get out of his system, and when he comes back he'll be the better for it, you wait and see. Being off by himself is going to help him straighten out."

But would they believe any of their words? Would they even believe they were worried? Or would the worry just be part of the surface, what they felt they *should* feel? And of course what he would have to get around to—not now, not now, getting drowsy with the rhythmic slap of the wipers, but some time later—is how *he* felt, if he felt anything at all. He closed his eyes, and soon the slap and the hum of the tires grew faint.

When he awoke, it was with the feeling that they had driven off the side of the road again; without opening his eyes, he hugged his sides and braced himself for the crash that would send him hurtling through the windshield, and for a split second saw himself lying on the highway, his body twisted into a grotesque sprawl, his tongue lolling out of his mouth.

The car stopped. "Well, we're here," Crow said. Howard opened his eyes. It was foggy outside. They had pulled off the highway onto a dirt road that ended near a clump of trees in a field of saw grass as high as the headlight beams, which skipped over the tips of the blades and reflected off the clinging water droplets. The beams penetrated into the grove of trees, whose thick trunks split into a canopy of branches that twisted against the dark sky. Howard had a sense of being near a river, but when he asked Crow, Crow only shrugged and said, "We're here. There's a path."

Crow snapped off the lights and got out, leading the way with a flashlight while Howard followed, carrying the large paper bag that had been in the back seat. The wet saw grass whispered against his knees. They came to the edge of the grove, walking in silence, and for fifty yards the path bordered the first row of trees, then cut to the right, then seemed to curve again so that Howard was unable to tell in which direction the highway was. Once he heard a truck moving through the night and the adhesive sound of tires on wet pavement, but the sounds were far away.

"Hold it!" Crow yelled suddenly. "Don't you move, Howie!" Howard had bent down to scratch his ankle. He stayed in that position. "Shit!" Crow said after a moment. "It's just a possum." Howard came up next to him and followed the flashlight beam. The possum's head lay several inches from its body, which had been slashed, unzipped down the middle, and gorged so that only a pouch of wet matted fur was left. "Almost stepped right on the thing, Howie." Crow continued to stare at the carcass. "Nothing could've done it but a hawk. You can always tell when the head's clean off like that. Boy, he really did a job, didn't he?"

Howard felt the mist washing over him, coating his skin. The field, the sky, the whole night seemed to be moving, enveloped in the shawl of the mist; and he felt himself being carried along and at the same time detached, fixed in a time away from the present, feeling that yesterday he might have said, "Tomorrow at this time you will be standing in a field with Crow Turner, looking at a dead animal." Or that next week or next year he would be able to say, "At that time, then, at that exact moment, Crow was pointing the flashlight into the belly of the ripped animal." And maybe then or yesterday there would be a feeling that it had happened or could happen, that he could reach out and touch Crow, touch the possum, smell the rotting pelt. Not now. Now they did not quite exist.

Crow kicked the head and body into the deep grass and started walking again. Howard's pant legs were soaked and clinging to his ankles. His eyes were beginning to sting. They walked on for a hundred yards, and the path cut sharply to the right so that again it bordered the trees.

And then in front of them, blocking the path, was an enormous tube. Its curved back arched above them, casting a shadow in the diffused beam of the flashlight, the long tube itself a shadow in the swimming mist. As they got closer Howard saw that a vast black curtain was draped over the tube. A metal snout protruded through an opening in the black curtain. The snout was torn open on one side to reveal a snarl of wires and cables wound about a rust-pocked block of iron. Above the snout a faint glow came through a window smeared with dark paint, and above the window on a strip of white paper behind a glass-enclosed slot was lettered the word CHARTERED.

Howard followed Crow around to the other side of the snout where Crow stopped. "Now you just take it easy, Howie." Crow stood there for a full minute, his back to Howard, his arms at his sides. The flashlight beam drilled into the wet ground. He made a noise in his throat and disappeared through the curtain into a soft orange light.

Howard took a step after him, then stopped. The wind had come up through the saw grass, plastering his shirt to him. Farther back in the night he heard the heavy rustling of the trees, and in front of him a metallic creaking came from beneath the curtain. A moment later there was a splinter of light at his feet, and Crow's head appeared through the curtain.

"It's okay, Howie; you can come in." They both waited, staring at each other. Howard hugged the paper bag. "I mean, you better come in now, Howie." Crow held the curtain apart, and Howard climbed up through it.

Inside there was a kerosene lamp hanging from the ceiling. There were rows of green leatherette seats, still intact although torn and spitting curlicues of horsehair. There was a smell of liquor and stale clothing. Around him Howard could hear the curtain flapping in the wind. Crow stood by the steering wheel. Without looking at him, Howard handed him the package. Between the rows of seats, the center aisle was littered with bottles and scraps of paper and food. Toward the back, just inside the perimeter of lantern glow, a man was sitting. Only his head and shoulders were visible. He wore a dark knit cap pulled down over his forehead and a blue denim shirt buttoned to the neck. His heavy, square jaw was black with a two- or three-day growth of beard. He sat there not moving, as if asleep, but his eyes caught the lantern flame and shot it back up the aisle in a red needle reflection that seemed to go right through Howard and Crow into the night.

Behind Howard, Crow stirred, slipped by him, and put the bundle in a seat across from the other man. "This is that fellow I was telling you about, Hubble." He hesitated and shuffled his feet. "I mean, he's just going to probably stay with us tonight." The man made no sign that he had heard. "I figured it wouldn't make any difference for one night. It'll be all right; I'll drive him back first thing in the morning. I've known this fella for a long time. I figured you wouldn't mind."

Hubble got up. He towered over Crow; the tassel of his cap brushed the metal ceiling. Now the lantern did not so much light up his face as absorb the glare of his skin which was stretched tight over wide cheekbones and a thick, flattened nose. He straddled the aisle, his hands grasping the backs of two seats. "Right now, Crow, I want to know how much money we got." His voice was deep, but flat and soft, as if the words had nothing to do with him, as if he were merely opening his mouth to let them escape.

"Money? Well, I mean, *you* got it, don't you? You always do, Hubble."

"That's right, I got the money." He changed the position of his hands. "But you know what I'm talking about, Crow; I'm talking about that list you been carrying around. You think maybe you remember what I'm talking about now?" By the steering wheel, Howard got a cigarette out of his shirt pocket, but did not light it.

"Oh, you mean that *list,* is that it?" Crow scratched the back of his neck. "Well, I still got it, Hubble. I sure do."

Hubble shot out a hand and grabbed Crow by the wrist. "You think you'll tell me then?" His voice was an explosion, and in the silence that followed Howard thought he heard something move at the far end of the aisle. There was a blanket stretched across the ceiling and hanging to the floor.

"Aw Hubble, I *got* it right here." Crow dug his free hand into his trouser pocket and brought out a folded brown piece of paper. Hubble let go of his wrist. "Let's see, Hub, you mean altogether, or just for Fort Worth? Well, altogether we got . . ." He hesitated and made a clicking sound with his tongue. "Altogether you should have ninety-three dollars in your pocket, Hub. Well, let's see, I don't mean ninety-three; I mean eighty-eight, because you gave five dollars to that night clerk, and then we made forty-five dollars last night. I mean we made forty-five that's part of the eighty-eight; I don't mean forty-five outside of it."

Hubble lit a cigarette, striking the wooden match on his belt buckle, and blew a stream of smoke toward the ceiling. "You sure of that?"

"Well . . . I'm sure. Let's see, we had sixty dollars . . ."

"All right." Hubble dropped the cigarette and stepped on it. "Forty-five goddam dollars."

"Forty-*four,*" Crow murmured, peering at the list. "We got

them hamburgers." Then, touching Hubble on the sleeve, he said, "That ain't too bad, Hub; it really ain't because there's only two other towns where we made more than that in a night. Let's see . . ." He studied the list again. "Let's see, we made sixty-five dollars in Abilene, but that was on account of the carnival. The only time we did better than that was in Wichita Falls on account of the air force being there, and even then we had to give ten dollars to that policeman; remember, Hubble, how he said he was going to arrest us for sure until you just kind of set that money down on the seat of his car, and then his saying, 'Okay boys, suppose I didn't even see you?' "

"Shut up, will you?" Hubble said, and Crow folded the list carefully and put it back in his pocket. "You think I don't know what the trouble is? You think maybe by some chance I haven't been knowing what's wrong right from the start?" He touched a scar above his eyebrow. "I'm going to change it."

Crow chanced a quick look at him. "Well, Hub, I'm *trying* my best, I am. I mean, it's my car, and that should count for something. And I did pretty good last night, making sure there wasn't trouble with the police and not messing with anyone unless I could see they was out for a good time."

"Nobody's talking about you, so don't get excited."

Crow laughed nervously. "Gee, I thought you were talking about *me*. You had me real worried because I *been* trying, and I been doing better lately. Right, Hubble? We're going to do all right, Hub, just like you said when I met you, remember? All you said you needed was a car; and me, I wasn't about to let nobody touch my car until you came along, but I knew we'd make a good team, Hubble—you and me."

"I want to know what time she passed out last night."

"Passed out? Well, let me see. I guess maybe after eight or nine. Yes, that was it; it was after nine times because, like you said I should do, I never left the room once. All the time I was in that closet, and every time one came in I checked it off on a piece of paper." Crow felt in his pocket again. "Well, I don't have it with me right now, Hub, but I remember making nine checks. The tenth one, when he came in I was all ready to make another check, and then, like I told you, he just kind of touched her and she rolled off onto the floor."

"I bet she did. I bet she rolled off onto that floor like a sack of mush."

Crow hesitated. "Well, she *did,* Hubble. I was right there watching all the time. I guess maybe it was pretty hot last night. I know staying in that closet all that time I was sweating like a pig."

Hubble lit another cigarette. "Yeah, well it ain't the heat that got her; it's that stuff she swilled down all day, and that's what's going to change."

Crow lit a cigarette too. "Well, Hub, I don't want you to believe *I'm* the one's been giving it to her. I don't even know where she gets it from, unless she makes some kind of deal with one of them fellas."

Hubble no longer was listening to him. He was looking over Crow's shoulder at Howard, who was still next to the steering wheel. He brushed past Crow and came up the aisle, stopping just in front of Howard. "Well, let's see, you're an old buddy of what's-his-name's, is that it?" He was standing with his arms at his sides, the cigarette stuck in a corner of his mouth.

Howard put a hand on the wheel. "I guess you could say we've known each other for a time, for maybe a few years."

Hubble nodded. "Yeah, that's what I said. Well, let me ask you this question, if it'd be all right; let me ask you what kind of match you think you are for him. You think who'd win between him and you if it'd come down to that?" Down the aisle, Crow coughed. "You think, for instance, you're a little smarter than him? I mean, I believe that fellow ain't the smartest one I ever met up with."

Howard waited a moment before he answered. "I guess I wouldn't know what to say to that. Crow's been around a lot. He's probably seen a lot of things that I don't know about."

"Yeah, well never mind. What are you doing now? What are you doing here?"

"I guess I'm not sure what I'm doing here."

"I guess you're not." Hubble hooked his thumbs in his belt, looked at Howard's face carefully for a minute, then began to laugh—at first a snort, like a stallion blowing air through his nostrils, then rocking back and forth on his heels, a deep guttural chuckle. It stopped abruptly and his arms dropped back to his sides. "Yeah, I'll tell you what you're doing: you're not doing nothing. What's your name, if you got one?"

Howard shuffled his feet. "Look, I'm pretty sure you know my name. I mean, when Crow came in, he must have . . ." He didn't finish. High above him, it seemed, Hubble's arm drew back as if reaching up to touch the ceiling, then descended slowly, gracefully, the huge fist sweeping in front of the orange lamp. There would have been time to move, time to have avoided the fist whose impact brought no pain, but was a sudden unbearable weight landing upon him. But he did not move because he had not even been watching Hubble. He had been watching someone far back down the aisle, under the arc of Hubble's arm. And now, reeling backward, his heels skittering on the floor, he struggled to raise his head from his chest and look over the length of his body which seemed to be rising in front of him, blocking his vision; and before he crashed into something hard that took away all light, he saw for another instant the naked girl with the golden hair who looked like Laura.

The staccato rasp of snapping metal punctured the night and rode in on a wave of white-hot stars that grew brighter as they billowed forth, grew to diamond brightness, then broke over the night and dispersed into black space. Another wave followed, rose, but did not so much break as blow apart. And the stars, instead of falling, hung in loose clusters, then flattened into a chain that slowly began to wind through the darkness, climbing, twisting, and suddenly dropping so that one end snapped up and fastened itself to the other. Now a circle, the star chain began to rotate, slowly at first, then more rapidly, until finally it turned so fast that clouds of stars were torn off; until all form was gone and in its place was unbearable brilliance.

Howard opened his eyes. He lay on his back on one of the leatherette seats, his feet hanging over into the aisle. Above him, the kerosene lamp flickered dimly and threatened to go out. The rasping sound continued, and Howard propped himself up on one elbow. Hubble was in the seat across the aisle, winding a clock; winding it slowly, carefully, so that each click was separate and distinct. He was leaning forward in the seat, his elbows resting on his knees. He held the clock with one hand between his legs and wound it with his thumb. Through a tear in the curtain, a strip of sunlight came in the window and fell across his knees.

"All right, then," Hubble said without looking up. "I don't believe I caught what the name is."

Howard told him.

"Yeah, well, what is it you said you think you're doing here?"

"I don't think I'm doing anything. I mean, I was just walking along the highway, and Crow came along and picked me up."

Hubble put the clock on the seat next to him. "Just walking along the highway, huh? At that time of night. You do that all the time?"

Howard sat up. As he did he felt pain at the base of his jaw just under his left ear, and with the pain he remembered. He pushed himself to his feet and took a step toward the blanket at the end of the aisle. Hubble's arm barred his way.

"Now you just sit down for a while. We're just getting started." He guided Howard back into the seat with one hand. "I believe you were about to tell me what you were doing out on the road."

Howard was still watching the blanket. "What difference does it make now? If you want to know the truth, I guess I was thinking about leaving town. I guess I was thinking there wasn't anything to do there any more." He spoke automatically, not really conscious of his words.

"Just what I figured," Hubble said. "You got the look. You think I couldn't tell all about you the first time I saw you?" He sat there for a moment, nodding his head, then reached out, grabbed the seat in front of him and pulled himself to his feet. "Listen, you little son of a bitch, don't come whining around here about having nothing to do. You expect there's supposed to be a lot of people waiting around to give you a break? You think everybody's some kind of relation to you, saying, 'Here's little what's-his-name again, we all better give him a little room, let him kind of ease into things nice and easy?' " He put his hands on his hips. "So now you come around here saying things are getting a little crowded for you, and maybe you think that's going to be news to me. Why don't you tell me something I don't know; I been crowded since the day I was born, and there ain't *nothing* to do except take care of yourself and give it to the rest of them before they give it to you." He looked at Howard a moment longer, then sat down again and lit a cigarette. "Why don't you tell me something I don't know?"

"Look, I didn't say all that. I just . . ." He stopped then, because the girl had come out from behind the blanket and was standing in front of it in the aisle. She had on a white dress.

It wasn't Laura, of course. Laura was somewhere safe in Hargrett—at home sitting on the porch or out with Burt. But the girl was blond, and her hair was long. The dress was a wrinkled satin evening gown whose discolored hem draped over her feet. There was a stain on the skirt, and a shoulder strap had fallen down over her arm; she was not really wearing the dress, but was only inside it. In the dim light her face was chalky. She stood there staring at Hubble, who did not look up. Then she went back behind the blanket.

"I don't believe I caught that last piece of information," Hubble said.

Howard took his eyes from the blanket and looked across the aisle. Hubble was watching him, his lips drawn back in a half smile. Howard felt sweat trickling down his sides.

"Never mind." Hubble laughed and stood up. "So you didn't believe there was much worth doing in that town. And you think the rest of the world's a lot different? You think your friend Crow's going to fix you up with a nice life?" He laughed again and rubbed a finger inside the border of the knit cap. "I don't believe he will." He walked slowly down the aisle and disappeared behind the blanket. Howard remained sitting.

A minute later Hubble and the girl came through the blanket. Hubble was wearing a peaked leather cap now and dark glasses. He held the girl by her arm. They came up the aisle slowly, the girl carrying a gold-spangled purse, her skirt trailing over the floor. The lantern was reflected in Hubble's glasses. As they went by him, Howard saw there was a thick layer of white powder on the girl's face. Particles of it were caught in her eyebrows, and it had caked at the corners of her mouth. Her eyes were closed. Just before they reached the steering wheel Hubble looked back over his shoulder. "If you're coming, come!" Then he and the girl went out through the curtain. Howard sat there watching the exposed piece of velvet sway. When it stopped, he got up.

They were ahead of him on the path. The sunlight had blinded him as he opened the curtain, and he had stumbled and fallen to his knees. Now, as he followed, he cupped one hand over his eyes for a visor. The sun was sucking all the rain out of the bushes and earth, and the earth steamed with the odor of rotted vegetation.

As the girl walked strands of mist disappeared in the folds of the satin skirt which glistened in the sun like wet skin. Hubble walked a few yards in front of her, not looking back to see if she was keeping up. But when she stumbled or stopped to pull a briar off her skirt he would slow his pace so that the same distance remained between them. As they neared the trees the girl tripped on a root or the hem of her skirt and fell face down. Behind her, Howard stopped and waited until she had gotten up. Ahead of her, Hubble cleaned his dark glasses.

The Hudson was parked near the border of trees. Crow was standing by it.

"Wait here," Hubble said to him. "I'll drive what's-his-name back."

"I can drive him, Hub. I know where he goes."

"You wait here. I got some things to do. I'll get you later."

Crow looked at Howard, then began to walk back toward the bus.

Hubble opened the rear door and the girl got in. He slammed the door with the back of his hand. "All right, let's go," he said to Howard.

Howard got in front and Hubble climbed in behind the wheel. When they had started down the path Hubble looked over at him. "Okay, sonny, if that little town of yours is looking pretty good to you about now, it don't matter a goddam to me. You understand what I'm saying? I'm saying you can stay or you can get the hell out of here; suit yourself." He lit a cigarette. "Only one thing makes any difference to me, and that's if you stay you do your job, and your job's anything I tell you, anything that helps get us through. And right now let's make sure you don't make any mistake about one thing; don't ever get it into your head that after a while you and Hubble are going to be good buddies, swapping stories and drinking beer. Because it ain't going to be like that, and don't think in a pinch I'm going to be any help to you. I don't even want to know what's going on inside your head, and you're not about to know what's going on in mine—and I don't believe *she's* going to have a lot to say."

Shrubbery scraped along the sides of the Hudson as it jolted over the path. Howard looked in the back seat. Only the girl's platinum head was visible. She had wrapped a soiled sheet around herself; under it her legs were moving slowly, rhythmically, her shoes scratching against the plastic seat cover.

They came to the edge of the highway, and the Hudson swung left on the blacktop which already wavered in pools of heat. Howard found a cigarette in his shirt pocket. He looked at Hubble. "What about Crow?" he said.

Hubble did not answer.

"What about Crow?" Howard repeated.

Hubble squinted down the road.

Part Two

IT WAS Shaylor's first night out since Howard had left. It had been a month. At two A.M. mist hung a few feet above the highway at headlight level; the dampness seeped through the floorboards and pressed against his chest as the truck raced on. He remembered that at his own wedding he had gotten two horses and a rig and had spent his wedding morning polishing the rig until it had shone like sunlight . . . and didn't he surprise everybody, and didn't he take Maggie's breath away!

I mean . . . all of us started out with hopes for the future and now all we have are hopes for the past; hope that it wasn't so bad as it seems, that even if things on the surface don't seem to add up to anything, if they look like failure, maybe there's something that came of it that we're not able to see and it wasn't really a failure. I mean, there was the land that betrayed us and we didn't count on that; we counted that that of course would be taken care of, and it stopped us and maybe it shouldn't have. But no one ever told us not to count on the land, and maybe the only thing you could pass on to somebody—to a son or a daughter—was that your life added up not to a guide but a warning. We counted on the land and we didn't even know about counting on ourselves; everything was taken care of except taking care of ourselves. And then there wasn't anything else left to do . . . except wait, wait for the son or daughter to make it up for you. But at least part of you—a small part of you that you don't even want to think about, but it's there, it's there all right—is waiting for *them* to fail just as bad as you did, *worse* than you did, so you can say, "There, you see what it's like? You see it's not just me?"

And they're waiting too; you bet they are . . . to use you as an example to follow. And part of *them* wants it to be a good one, something they can carry with them and make into their own pride; but, just like you, part of them is wanting it to be a bad example so they can say, "At least I'm better than *he* is; at least I'm not failing the same way *he* did." Then you get tired of waiting; you get tired of the whole thing.

In the fog one hundred and forty miles northeast of Hargrett a twelve-ton silver trailer truck geared down and descended the exit ramp of the elevated highway into the outskirts of the city. It cruised along the narrow service road which merged into a residential street whose wet blacktop reflected the yellow glow of the streetlamps. At the first intersection the truck turned right, the cab cornering smartly, the long trailer sweeping gently around the curve as the truck proceeded between rows of squat apartment buildings and one- and two-story houses. Now it turned left in its course, its red taillights disappearing for an instant in a puff of mist, then emerging. From back yards the truck was a shadowy moving bridge, momentarily linking one house to the next; from the cab the headlight beams were diffused by the fog, picking out on front lawns an upended bicycle, metal chairs, a garden hose curled over a tree limb. The truck made one more right turn, then headed east. It stopped, hissing, for a blinking red signal. In a second-story window of a corner apartment building there was a light. The shade was part way up; and there was someone standing near the window. The truck moved out.

"We ought to go to bed soon, Laurie. We've got all day tomorrow and Sunday to finish arranging things." Burt moved away from the window and sat down on the arm of a new easy chair. He lit a cigarette and put the burnt-out match in his shirt pocket.

"But I'm not really tired. Let's just stay up a little while longer. We could try putting the couch against the back wall and maybe the chair kitty corner over near the lamp; I think it might look nice there." Laura finished straightening a watercolor painting of the Tower of London that Grace Cowley had given them. She was wearing blue jeans and an old Hargrett High sweatshirt of her brother's. Her hair was pulled back and fastened with a rubber band. "It's just that I want it to be right, Burt; I want it to be the kind of home that when people come to visit us they'll know right away that everything really belongs. Monday I'm going to look at rugs. We don't have to get wall-to-wall, but . . ." She broke off and went over to Burt. That morning, waiting for the furniture to be delivered, sitting in the middle of the empty living room, she remembered the nights in Hargrett when she had lain in bed thinking of how it would be when she lived in a house of her own, and remembered that once the four of them had been driving somewhere at night and had passed a solitary house whose front windows, both upstairs and down, were filled with light. She couldn't see in; the house was set back too far from the highway, but that night and later nights she would fall asleep furnishing the house until every detail of every room was fixed in her mind. It had come back to her only then in the empty living room; she had not thought of the house when she and Burt were picking out furniture. "It's just that I want it to be right," she said. "Does that sound silly?"

Burt stood up and took her in his arms. "It sounds fine. Do you know what *I* want? I want exactly what you do. And that's why we're really lucky. I mean, the way I figure it there are a lot of people who start out together not even knowing if they want the same things out of life. Look at our parents, maybe not yours as much as mine, but you can't help wondering how two people can get married and live together for a long time and neither of them know what the other one really wants out of life."

Laura leaned against him. Was that it? Was that the way it had been with her parents? Then all their living in the past was meaningless, and they had not really lost something because they never had anything to begin with. And for all the watching, the careful watching of each other and the fears that all four of them held for each other, they were all really strangers to each other. But maybe Burt was wrong; maybe her father and mother *had* started out wanting the same thing and then something had happened to make one or both of them change. Her father had lost the ranch; wouldn't that have been enough to make them change? But then why hadn't their loss brought them closer together? There must have been something else. Or maybe it was that over the years each changed a little bit at a time without either of them noticing until they were no longer the same people. But if this were it, why? And if it had happened to them . . .

"But we're not going to be like that, Laurie, because I know where I'm going, I really do. And we're going to have the things we want—a nice house and enough money so we won't have to worry, and a family we can take care of so they won't have to worry either. We *are* going to have all these things because we're going to do it by planning, not making all the mistakes those other people do who end up with nothing except feeling sorry for themselves." He patted her shoulder and smiled. "Well, I didn't mean to start sounding off. The only thing I really wanted to say is that you're safe here, Laurie. You don't have to worry about anything because everything is going to be taken care of."

Laura had been staring out the window at the blinking light suspended over the street. Now she looked at her husband. Because he was strong she would believe him. They *wouldn't* be trapped in the fear and bitterness of Hargrett. They could be free of it. If they were careful, they could be free.

Burt kissed her on the cheek. "Now let's go to bed. No sense in getting all tired out."

"All right." She touched his sleeve. "I was just thinking about Howie."

Burt smiled. "I wouldn't worry about him; he can take care

of himself. Didn't your folks get a letter from him a while back?"

"A postcard, but that was three weeks ago, and he didn't say anything except that he was all right."

"Well he *is* all right. Look, I know a lot of fellas who just took off on their own for a while. I almost thought of doing it myself once. It'll probably do him a lot of good, and when he comes back you know what he'll want to do? He'll want to find a good job and start thinking about getting married and settling down. That's the truth, Laurie. You wait, once he puts his mind to it he'll see what's important. Howie's a smart boy. Maybe he'll even go into the army; that'd be good for him. But if it'll make you feel better, when he gets back he can stay with us for a while and I'll put him onto a couple of job leads if he wants to settle down around here." Burt snapped off the lamp and, with his arm around her, led Laura into the bedroom.

"This real estate dealer came into the office today," Burt said as they were undressing; "a fella we sold a liability policy. You know what he said you can do? You can make a down payment on a lot even if you don't plan to build on it for a while, and then just make monthly payments so that by the time you *are* ready to build the lot might be all paid for."

Laura was in the bathroom. She undid the rubber band and combed out her hair. On the plastic rack near the sink hung two blue bath towels with pink initials, L. S. C. They were from Burt's mother. "We haven't even really moved in here yet; don't you think it's too soon to be thinking about buying land for a house?"

Burt took off his shoes and lined them up on the floor of his closet. "Well, of course we're going to stay here. This is perfect for now. But the way I figure it, starting to make payments now would be a good investment for the future. I mean, I know we still have to pay for the furniture but that doesn't take too much of a bite each month, and in a couple of years the value of land will probably go up quite a bit. We might not be able to find as good a deal as we could now." He draped his socks over the back of a chair. "Also, if our plans change and we decide not to build on the lot we could always sell it at a profit." Laura came out of the bathroom. She was wearing a black knee-length nightgown with a white lace frill at the neck, a gift from Gail Batts who had sat next to her in social studies. "Anyway," Burt said, "it's just a thought. Maybe someday just for the fun of it we could drive around a couple of the lots. They're out in the Parkhurst area; it's nice out there." He went into the bathroom and closed the door. Laura went over to the doorway and looked into the living room.

That morning after the delivery men had uncrated the furniture she had spent more than two hours sitting first in one chair, then the other and then the couch, trying to get used to them as quickly as possible, trying to make them a part of herself. New things were wonderful because no one had ever used them before; no one's memories were part of them. Things that belonged only to you could make you feel independent . . . and free.

Later, in bed with the lights out, she nestled her head in the hollow of Burt's shoulder. "It's just that I'm so excited about having a place of our own right here that I can't even think about ever moving."

"I know." Burt put his lips against her forehead. "It was just talk anyway." His hand pressed the small of her back. "Are you happy, Laurie? I am. We're just starting out and things are gonna get even better for us." His hand caressed her thighs and moved up over her stomach to stroke her breasts. "You're my sweet wife and I love you."

"I love you too, Burt; I do."

He undid the buttons of her nightgown and slipped the gown from her shoulders, his mouth seeking her breast, his hand now between her thighs.

"Let me get up," Laura whispered, "just for a minute."

"It's all right, Laurie."

"No, please; just for a minute. We shouldn't take the chance."

"It's all right. It's what we want; we don't have to wait." His body pressed down on her. His knees held her thighs apart.

"Burt, not yet! Please, not yet!" Burt seemed not to hear her. She struggled to move from under him, but though she clawed at the sheet her outstretched arm could not reach the edge of the new maple bed. "Oh God, Burt, please!"

And then he was inside her. His shoulder was against her cheek as he pulled her hips to him in quickening rhythm. "It's all right, Laurie; it's all right, it's all right."

The prison of his arms held her tight. Only later, when he lay relaxed on top of her, did she hear her own scream in the dark room and feel the sudden chill that came over her body.

On the desert floor in the early morning a six-foot gopher snake uncoiled and began to glide slowly in and out of the spiny stems of the pygmy scrub, its thick body flowing forward and into itself like a stream of dusty mud, its tongue flicking the air. Giant grasshoppers rose zipping in the snake's path to hover in the air. A black-and-yellow scorpion scuttled over the floor, its newly born young clinging like maggots to its back. From a hole near the base of a mesquite bush a young jackrabbit emerged to sit on its haunches and blink into the new light. It was a frozen animal in the sun; for several minutes it remained still, holding its short front legs delicately over its chest. Its only movement was the quivering of its nose and the soft blinking of its eyes. Then, at once, even this movement stopped and a different stillness came over the animal, a tense waiting silence that stiffened its entire body. The rabbit shivered, dropped to all fours, and darted. But the flattened head of the gopher snake struck into the loose flesh at the nape of the rabbit's neck, knocking the animal off its feet and sending it sprawling against the horny scrub stems, while with its fangs still hooked deep into the flesh the snake lashed the ground like an electric wire, its tail scratching a scalloped fan into the dust. On its back, saliva streaming from its nose and mouth, the rabbit thrashed from side to side, its legs clawing at the air. But now the electric snake drove again and again, its head blurred with speed, now driving at the throat and winding its body around the rabbit; the snake and the rabbit rolled against the scrub in a shuddering embrace, stirring up dust until both animals were hidden. Then, propelled by the rabbit's final spasm, they rode up through the dust clouds, the snake entwined about the rabbit, and for a split second they hung motionless before dropping.

Later, bloated, the gopher snake pulled itself over the sand, its body undulating in sluggish figure S's. Then slowly, carefully, as if not to puncture itself on the pebbles, it streamed down the bank of the ditch that ran along the edge of the highway. On the road shoulder the snake paused, head raised, before it flowed forward onto the blacktop which already simmered in the eight o'clock sun. Now halfway across the road with its snout just over the white line, the snake stopped again, then thrust its head forward. The rest of its body followed, the S's smaller, rapid. But the macadam was slippery under its belly, and the short rapid thrusts carried the snake not only forward but sideward. And before its tail was across the line, the snake was smeared under the wheels of a fast-moving car heading south.

They had pulled out of MacGregor at six A.M. Sunday morning with Hubble driving, Howard curled up in the front seat next to him and the girl asleep in back, covered by the sheet. By eight, with the sun already floating red on the rim of the horizon, they were a good hundred and fifty miles on the road, Hubble pushing the car to its limit. There were no other cars yet, just the Hudson cutting through the middle of the flatland, scooting down the highway like a metallic bug looking for some place to bury itself.

Hubble looked over at Howard and into the rear view mirror, then took a cigarette from his shirt. His long body was cramped behind the wheel, and behind the sunglasses his eyes shifted from one side of the road to the other. The cigarette stayed in his mouth; he worked it with his lips, the smoke floating up into his face, clinging to his beard, settling under the visor of his leather cap.

Ten miles later they passed their first car, a dust-caked sedan belching smoke from its exhaust and hugging the road shoulder. Inside, an elderly couple dressed in Sunday clothes sat erect and stared straight down the center of the highway.

As if this were a signal, Hubble jabbed Howard's shoulder. Howard pulled his knees up to his chest, curling into a tighter ball, and moved closer to the window. Hubble poked him again and shook him by the collar. "Okay," Howard mumbled, "okay."

"Wake up!"

Howard rubbed his hands over his face and straightened up, leaning against the door. He opened his eyes for a second, then closed them against the sunlight. "Okay, what is it?"

"Here." Hubble put the cigarette between Howard's lips. "I want to know how much money we got."

Howard took one drag and threw the butt out the window without opening his eyes. He slumped back down in the seat. "You got the money."

"You think maybe I don't know who got the money? I'm talking about that list." The sun was level with the car now, and the grasshoppers buzzed against the windshield, giving voice to the heat that already made the hood waver as if it were floating independently of the rest of the car.

Howard reached into his trouser pocket and pulled out a scrap of paper. "We got sixty-eight dollars," he said after a moment.

"Sixty-eight. That's what I figured."

"Where are we heading for?"

"You just don't worry about that; I'll take care of where we're heading for. You just worry about keeping that list of expenses straight and keeping your eyes open for trouble. That's all you got to do until I tell you different." They drove on in silence, the heat from the road blowing back through the motor and up inside their trouser legs. Before Howard closed his eyes again he looked in the back seat. The sheet had slipped, exposing the girl's legs and the hem of her gown. From under the sheet there came a faint sucking noise. Howard could smell liquor, but Hubble did not seem to notice.

When Howard awoke the car was parked in a gas station next to the pump, and Hubble was standing in front of the car looking in with the sun reflecting off the top of his cap. Howard stared back at him, not fully awake, remembering that once somewhere he had seen the head of a fly magnified hundreds of times so the eyes seemed waiting to envelop you, waiting for you only to touch them and be swallowed in their soft black centers. Howard rubbed his eyes. When he looked up again Hubble was walking toward the station house. Howard got out of the car and leaned against a fender.

The house was a one-room tin-roofed shack that once had had a coat of whitewash, but now, except for a few scabs of paint, was burned ash gray by the sun. Strips of burlap hung in the window, and over the doorway was a poster of a boy in pajamas with his arm hooked through an enormous tire. A fat man wearing coveralls and a khaki undershirt came out the door. Hubble pointed at the car, and the fat man scratched himself and nodded.

"How far are we?" Howard asked, coming around the car to stand by Hubble. The man cranked the pump and unwound the gas hose.

Hubble struck a wooden match against the side of the doorway and lit a cigarette, then squatted and scooped up a handful of gravel, letting it slide through his fingers. "Twenty miles from Dandelion; forty miles from Wyandotte."

"Wyandotte's where we're going?"

"That's right." The man shook the nozzle of the hose and Howard started back toward the car, but Hubble grabbed him by the belt and pulled himself up. Howard waited beside him.

"Is that all?" The fat man stood in front of them, his arms folded loosely across his belly.

"Yeah, that's all." Hubble smiled.

"It'll be four-sixty. I checked the oil; it's okay."

"You look at the radiator?"

"Water's all right too."

"Then I guess we're all set. Wouldn't you say we were all set, mister?"

"What do you mean?" The man unfolded his arms.

"I mean my friend here and me been on a long trip, traveling for a long time, and we're both kind of short of cash at the moment."

"You ain't planning to pay for the gas?"

Hubble smiled again. "Credit," he said, "credit."

The fat man was silent. He looked at Hubble's face, then at Howard, then walked carefully around them and disappeared into the shack. Hubble shoved Howard in the direction of the car.

Howard was driving now. Hubble lounged in the seat next to him, one knee propped up against the dashboard. "I suppose you're feeling sorry for that fat boy back there, figuring he's just a poor son of a bitch minding his own business, probably with a wife and a brat on his neck, and along comes somebody like us and screws him out of a big sale."

"We could have paid him," Howard said. "It was only four-sixty."

"Yeah, we could've but we didn't. But don't you worry about fat boy; he'll make it up on the next one. Next one pulls in for gas, fat boy'll just happen to spot one of his shock absorbers is busted or his wheels are out of line. 'Say, fella, it's pretty dangerous driving a car in that condition.' And the guy'll drive away thinking fat boy's done him a real favor instead of giving him a screwing."

The early-morning clouds had disappeared, and the sky was beginning to whiten as the sun climbed higher and the shadows of the telegraph poles grew shorter. Howard flipped the sun visor down. "You can't be sure he's going to do that. Not everybody operates that way."

Hubble spat out the window. "Tell me about it; tell me about all the ones who don't. No, don't bother; just shut up for a while. I got some things to think about."

They passed a sign that said, "You are ten miles from Claude Ring the Watermelon King," and another that said, "The First Baptist Church of Dandelion Welcomes You," and then Hubble said, "What do you think about what's-her-name?" He inclined his head toward the back seat.

"What do you mean? I don't think anything about her. I mean, she isn't any of my business."

Hubble laughed. "Yeah, that's the way. You get the idea fast, don't you? Well, never mind; it don't make any difference. The only thing that matters is that before too long she's going to be your little bride; as a matter of fact, not any longer than it takes us to get to Dandelion."

Howard looked over at Hubble slowly. "What do you mean?"

"I got somebody in Dandelion who'll get us a marriage license in case anybody wants to know."

Howard's hands tightened on the steering wheel. "I don't know what you're talking about, but I'm not going to be any part of that. I'm not marrying anyone." He turned the wheel sharply to avoid a clump of sagebrush in the center of the highway. In the back seat the girl moaned softly.

"Is that right?" Hubble picked a shred of tobacco from between his teeth. "Well, you're part of it! You're part of it at that gas station back there and you're part of it every night when the stiffs come up paying their five bucks for what's-her-name; and you're part of it because you want to be, so don't talk to me about going to be anything, understand what I'm saying? I'm saying the rules ain't changed, and as long as you stay around you do a lot of the listening and I'll do a lot of the talking." He lit a cigarette and blew a stream of smoke at the dashboard. "Before you start jumping out of your skin, it's only a piece of paper I'm talking about, something to show she's married to one of us in case anybody starts snooping around in Wyandotte."

Howard relaxed his hands on the wheel. "You mean it's just a certificate we'd have if we ever need it."

"That's right."

"Well, uh . . . couldn't it be *you* instead of *me* that was married to her? I mean, since it doesn't really matter." He studied the white center line. "Not that it makes any difference to me."

"Good," Hubble said, "because it's got to be you because you got the driver's license in case anybody feels like checking who you are." He flipped the cigarette out the window, and Howard knew there wasn't going to be any more talk about it.

They were on the outskirts of Dandelion now, and Howard eased off the accelerator as they passed the tarpaper shacks and rusted automobiles that crowded each side of the road. It was nine-thirty, and young Mexican girls in church-white dresses walked along the sand path at the highway's edge, carrying their shoes with two fingers. Hubble allowed his eyes to flick over them as they drove by, but Howard looked straight ahead, his eyes narrowed; and it was not until they had parked on a side street of town behind the courthouse and Hubble had gone that he took his hands from the steering wheel and lit a cigarette.

In it because he *wanted* to be? It hadn't seemed to be a matter of wanting to be here; not a conscious action that had taken him from Hargrett and his family to separate him from them not by miles or weeks, but by an incalculable distance over which there was no bridge between that town, that house, and the gutted remains of an abandoned bus, or a hotel room in Belton or MacGregor, or a sun-blasted highway that existed only unto itself without reference to time or space and on which he had lost the voice of a son or a brother or a one-night lover.

"If you'd be kind enough to give me a cigarette, I might tell you a secret." For a moment Howard thought the whisper had been in his own mind. He turned to the back seat. The girl was lying on her back now, and the damp sheet tucked under her chin had ridden up over her thighs, pulling her skirt with it and exposing the chalky flesh above her stocking tops. Above the sheet her powdered face in the sunlight was a mask collecting dust. Her waxy-blue eyelids were lowered, but behind the lashes Howard could see her eyes moving. He held a cigarette out to her but she remained motionless. Then suddenly she was staring directly at him, her eyes opened wide.

"What the hell do you want, you fucking son of a bitch?" She looked at him a moment longer, then her expression changed and she reached out and took the cigarette. Howard lit it for her, and she lay back and watched the exhaled smoke curl toward the roof. "Sorry; I wake up nervous sometimes when I see a stranger." Her voice was a whisper again. "But you're not a stranger really, are you? You've been along." Howard nodded. "Have you been along always? I'm no good with faces, but you see, I remember you now." She touched her hair. "You see, I've seen your face at different times, but it's difficult to know how long. You see . . ." Her voice trailed off and she flicked an ash on the seat.

"It's only been a little while."

"Yes. Then you never at any time got caught fucking me, did you?"

Howard shook his head.

She raised herself up on one elbow. "Does that mean you did not, or that you don't remember if you did?"

"No, I never did." Out the rear window Howard saw a police car approaching. It drove slowly past the Hudson and turned right at the corner. He took the cigarette from her and dropped it out the window. "It wasn't me," he said, his voice tight in his throat. "Was it Crow? Is that what happened?"

"Crow?" The girl laughed. "I never fucked a crow." From under the sheet she pulled out an empty liquor bottle. "Look, would you be kind enough to step outside and bring me back a fresh one of these? I believe it would just take you a minute and then I would be glad to reimburse you. I would be more than glad to reimburse you for your trouble."

"I'm sorry; I can't. I've got to stay in the car." He lit another cigarette and handed it to her. "Besides, it's Sunday."

"I can drink on Sunday."

"I know, but you can't buy it. The liquor stores are all closed."

"You could try a house," she said faintly. "You could knock on someone's door and say it's an emergency." She sighed and pulled the sheet down over her knees.

"My name is Howard."

"Is it?" She kicked the bottle off the seat. "It could be worse; it could be Barbara Jo."

"Is that your name?"

"Like shit it is! You can call me Regal."

"I will then. It's a nice name."

"I gave it to myself." Her giggle ended in a choke. "Get it? Gave it to myself." Howard took the cigarette from her. "He liked it too."

"Who?"

She made no answer. Her eyes were closed again.

"Who was it that liked your name?" Howard tried to keep his voice even. "Was it anyone I know? *Was* it?"

She spoke slowly. "It's none of your fucking business."

Howard put his feet up and leaned against the door. "Look, I'll run out and get a cold drink if you're thirsty, but I'd better not right now. I'll do it when Hubble gets back." Across the square three old men sat on a bench under the eaves of the two-story wooden St. Regis Hotel. "What was it you were going to tell me if I gave you a cigarette?"

"Nothing. I was going to tell you it if you got me a drink, mister; that's what I really meant. Who cares about a cigarette?"

Howard sat up and leaned over the back seat. "You don't *have* to tell me; I know already. It was Crow, wasn't it? It was Crow who liked your name. That's why Hubble left him; you don't have to tell me. He thought the two of you might try something."

While he was speaking Regal sat up and watched him, squinting into the sunlight, her hair matted against the nape of her neck. Now she lay back again and pulled the sheet over her head. Howard watched the sheet ripple where her mouth was against it. He waited for her to speak, but she said nothing. And then the sheet began to shake, and from under it came a squeal of laughter. "There *was* someone else along and it wasn't you. It was a crow and I remember, but . . ." Her voice dropped so that Howard could barely hear her. "But it wasn't him who got caught. You see, I remember now; but you see, the trouble is I can't remember who it was who . . . crow!" She laughed again. "You don't know anything, do you? You're so stupid. Even I know you just have to scare a crow and it flies away."

Howard stared at her as if he were trying to see through the sheet. "What do you mean?"

"She means you shoot off your mouth a lot about something you don't know anything about." Howard whirled around. Hubble was standing by the door looking in. "You got it all figured out, don't you?" He got in behind the wheel. "Christ, that piece of nothing! You think he matters to anybody? I thought you might be able to keep your mouth shut and pay attention to what we're doing, but you're just as dumb as the other one, aren't you?" Hubble started the car, shifted into gear and hooked a right turn back onto the highway. In the back seat, Regal was silent.

When they got to Wyandotte, it wasn't much different from Dandelion except for the soldiers. The streets were wider and the courthouse bigger, but it was still the same—the business section strung out in a quadrangle with the courthouse in the center—and it could have been a lot of towns in the southwest except for the soldiers. The soldiers walked along the sidewalks in pairs and groups, hands in pockets, wearing flowered sport shirts or knit jerseys, and once in a while a summer khaki uniform.

Hubble drove around the square slowly, one arm out the window, his fingers tapping lightly against the side of the car. There were more soldiers inside the bus terminal, playing the pinball machines or just sitting on the wooden benches, smoking and listening to the juke box. Farther up the street music belched out of Shirley's Lounge and the New Paradise Café. Fifteen or twenty soldiers were stretched out on the lawn of the courthouse listening to a portable radio.

They drove around the square twice, Howard not even looking up, just staring at the dashboard, and Hubble whistling softly under his breath and drumming his fingers against the door; then they pulled up to the curb in front of the Wyandotte Belle Hotel. Hubble switched off the ignition, stretched and turned to Howard.

"Okay. Now I'm going to do all the talking when we get in there so you don't have to say anything; so you just listen to what I'm saying and hold onto her till we get up to the room because I'm not planning to have any trouble." Howard didn't answer, only moved his head to one side so Hubble would know he was listening. "Okay," Hubble said, "let's go."

He got out and opened the door and looked in at Regal who was still covered. Hubble peeled off the sheet. "All right, we're ready." She didn't open her eyes. "I said we're ready." He put his hand on her shoulder and shook her a couple of times. Regal opened her eyes for an instant, then closed them again. Hubble straightened up, looked both ways down the sidewalk, then leaned in and pulled her up to a sitting position. "Okay," he said to Howard, who was standing behind him, "right into the hotel and let's not waste any time doing it." He grabbed Regal by one arm and the back of her neck and pulled her out of the car, Howard reaching out to hold her other arm as she began to fall; supporting her between them, Hubble and Howard went up the porch steps and into the hotel lobby.

For a moment they stood inside the doorway. Howard blinked, adjusting his eyes to the dim lavender room which was lighted only by rays of sunlight slanting in between the oilcloth curtains of a corner window. Straight-backed maple chairs lined one wall; except for the room clerk's desk near the stairway, there was no other furniture. In the center of the lobby a cactus plant was stuck into a concrete urn. They stood there and then Regal began to sway, and Hubble pulled her up straight, brushing her hair back from her face with his free hand. He looked at Howard, nodded, and they started toward the desk.

The desk clerk was a soft white balding man with a green eyeshade. He looked up when he heard the floor creak, sat up erect, and when they got within six feet of the desk, stood quickly and took off the eyeshade. His arms below the wilted short-sleeved shirt were pale and freckled. His look darted from one face to another, settled on Regal, then dropped to the desk.

Hubble smiled. "You got a double room in front for my friend here and his bride?" He took a cigarette from his shirt and struck the match on the desk top. "They just got married," he continued in a confidential tone. "That's why she's so tired—too much partying last night, if you know what I mean." There was a red welt across the clerk's forehead where the shade had been.

"Look, I don't want any trouble with anybody."

Hubble reached into his pocket and put three five-dollar bills on the desk. "There ain't going to be any trouble. I got a marriage license in case anybody wants to see it."

The clerk looked at the money. "You planning to have a lot of soldiers in here?" He raised his eyes to a level with Hubble's belt.

"No, not a lot. Just one at a time. And there ain't going to be any noise."

The clerk looked at Regal again and rubbed the back of his neck. "No noise," he said, picking up the money. He took a key from the rack, handed it to Hubble, then sat down again and put on the eyeshade. "Room 2-B."

The three of them went up the stairs, Regal's toes scraping on each step, and as they reached the second floor one of her shoulder straps fell away so that Howard could see her breast. He looked away from her quickly and down the narrow hall. And then, as Hubble peered at each door number, Regal began to hum softly to herself, just loud enough for Howard to hear. He tried to whistle, but it didn't work; his lips were too dry and he could still hear her. He looked past her at Hubble to see if he was paying any attention, but then they were in front of 2-B, and Howard took away his hand so that Regal slipped out of Hubble's grasp and fell to the floor at the base of the corridor wall.

"Look," Howard said before Hubble had a chance to speak, "I don't have to stay here any more, you know. I'm free to go. There's something going on here and I don't even mean the way you make your money; that's your own business, and if someone wants to pay you and her for it, it doesn't make any difference to me. But there's something going on between you and her that's different from everything else. I don't even think it's got anything to do with Crow; maybe you were telling the truth about him. But there's something else that's happening here!"

Hubble turned the dark glasses toward him, then looked down at Regal who was playing with the hem of her skirt. He unlocked the door, bent down and picked her up, and disappeared into the room. A moment later he was back in the hall. He grabbed Howard by the front of the shirt, pulled him into the room, and slammed the door shut with his foot. He slapped Howard once, then jammed him against the wall. "It's business is all!" he shouted, his face a few inches from Howard's. "We drive around to towns and we get guys to fuck her for money; and if I tell you to, you do some of the driving and keep your eyes open to see there ain't any trouble, and that's all it is!" He slapped him again and the dark glasses bore in. "I told you the only reason you're here is because I thought you could handle yourself better than the other one. Nobody needs any of your goddam ideas; I told you that." He dropped his arms to his sides. "Leave?" he said softly. "You wouldn't leave if I paid you to; you think I don't know that?" He stood in front of Howard a moment longer, then turned away and walked over to the window and looked out. "What are you talking about? What's going on inside your head?"

Howard hadn't moved; he stood with his spine pressed against the wall. On the bed, Regal rolled over onto her stomach so that one leg hung over the edge of the mattress, her foot just touching the green throw rug.

Hubble walked back over to the door. "Okay. I'll tell you what's going to happen. You're going to stay right here and you're going to see she don't pass out. And when I get ready to send the first one up I'm going to send him, and she's going to be ready, you see what I mean?" He put his hand on the doorknob. "And any time you want to say anything to me, just go on and say it, see what I mean? And if maybe you don't like the way things are going, well, you know . . ." he opened the door ". . . change them." Suddenly he wheeled around and looked at Regal, then at Howard. "What do you think she is?" he shouted. "Just what the fuck do you think she is?" He stood there for a moment, then went out the door and slammed it behind him.

Howard waited until he could no longer hear Hubble's footsteps in the hall. Without looking at Regal he went over to the window. He could see into Shirley's Lounge across the street. There were soldiers sitting along one wall on battered picnic benches and at small, round-topped tables clustered in the middle of the café. But no one sat for long; there was a constant movement of soldiers getting up to refill their glasses, put coins into the bubbling green juke box by the window, or just stand snapping their fingers to the beat of the electric guitar music. A cloud of cigarette smoke hung in the sunlight outside the door where two soldiers were dancing together, each clutching a bottle of beer.

Hubble was on the curb now, in front of the hotel steps. He waited there for several minutes looking across the street, his hands stuffed in his back pockets; then he crossed over. From the window Howard watched him elbow his way into the café and up to the bar. A heavy blond woman behind the bar came over to stand in front of him. A moment later she brought him a bottle of beer. Hubble took one swallow from it, turned and leaned against the bar on his elbows. He was partly hidden from Howard's sight by a post in the center of the café floor, but Howard could see that he stayed in that position for several minutes before he leaned over and said something to the soldier who was standing next to him.

Howard turned away from the window. He would stay. Maybe he had known it since the time they had driven off from the bus; maybe what had come to the surface was just his final weak outcry against his own entrance into Hubble's stripped world where the failures of Hargrett became only failures of those dying before they were born, whose lives had taken them just far enough to invent a past that would kill the present and future. Unless they were fat men in overalls who would make it up on the next one who came along. And what he had come upon in the hall in that instant of horror and excitement was not something that existed between Hubble and Regal, but only the consciousness that because he, as Hubble had done, was stripping himself of both hope and despair, he would survive. He leaned against the window sill. "Belong here, Miss Cowley?" he said softly, "belong here?"

"What you don't even know, mister, is that he needs you just like you need him, and you better not go around saying things like you did or you'll start some kind of trouble for sure." Regal had rolled over; she lay on her side watching him. She had perspired through her make-up, and in the bright room granules of powder caked her face like stucco. Her hair fell over one shoulder; where it was parted in the center of her head, dark-brown roots sliced through the platinum. "He won't like it if you spoil things."

Howard went over and sat down in a chair next to the bed. "What do you mean, he needs me? And who said anything about me needing him? I got along pretty well before this, and I don't believe it's going to break anyone's heart—his or mine—when I decide to take off."

Regal laughed. "Sure, you got along just fine; that's why you're here." She got the pillow out from under the bedspread and hugged it to her. "I'll tell you what I'm going to do. If you would just be kind enough to run downstairs and get about a fifth of blended, I would be grateful enough to relate to you the entire story of my life. You see, it would only take a minute for you to get it because when we were on the way in here I just happened to notice there was one of those stores next door. I know you'd be interested in my life story."

Howard didn't answer. He got a cigarette out of his shirt pocket.

Regal began to rock back and forth, the pillow in her arms. "Now why is it every time I ask you for just one small favor you have to smoke a crummy cigarette?"

"I told you before, you can't buy it on Sunday."

She stroked the pillow. "Where there's a will there's a way." She lay there looking at him for a moment, then suddenly sat up and threw the pillow at him. "You think I'm as stupid as to have to rely on you for anything?" She laughed and tossed her hair. "That was just a damn test, you dumb Howie or whatever your name is, just a damn test to see what kind of a shit you'd be!" She reached under the spread, not taking her eyes from him, and brought out an unopened half-pint of whisky. "See that? Now what can you say about that? It ain't much, I admit, but it's something and it's something I can get any old time I want. You just put that in your goddam cigarette and smoke it." She unscrewed the top and took several swallows from the bottle. "Now you can give me one of those things if you like." Howard lit another cigarette and handed it to her. "But you'll have to excuse me if I don't offer you anything in return." She put the bottle to her lips again and tilted her head back, the tendons in her throat straining as she drank. She lowered the bottle again and examined it. "See, it goes fast." The whisky was more than half gone.

Howard leaned forward in the chair. "What did you mean before about him needing me?"

"Nothing," she laughed. She took another swallow, then lowered the bottle slowly and held it in her lap. "Except he needs a witness and you're it. He had that friend of yours for a while, but he was too dumb to be much good and now he's got you."

"What do you mean?"

"What d'you mean? What d'you mean?" Regal repeated in a high-pitched voice. She stubbed out her cigarette on the headboard and lay back, the neck of the bottle pressed against her cheek. "I mean it wouldn't work if it was just me." She tilted the bottle to her mouth. A trickle of whisky ran down her chin and throat. "He's got to have somebody like you around every minute of the day so everybody knows just where they stand. Get it?" She giggled. "No, you wouldn't get it in a million years. He couldn't do it if it was just me and him." She sucked up the last of the whisky and let the bottle slide out of her hand onto the floor. "But what about you, little man? What kind of a witness are you going to be?" She stretched lazily and kicked off her shoes. "You know you'd better be careful. You heard what he said about not letting me pass out." She smiled. "Know the best way to make sure? Best way in the world?" She winked at Howard and began to stroke her thighs. "Sure, that's it; why not? That's what I'm here for and you're along for the ride, so why not get the best ride you can, know what I mean?"

Howard stood up. "Thanks just the same. Maybe some other time."

"What's the matter, you afraid of me?" Regal raised one leg and pointed her toes at the ceiling. Her skirt rode up over her thighs. "I could show you some things. I could really show you some things you'd like." Her voice had become husky and she swung her leg in rhythm with her words. "That's what I'm here for, that's what I'm really good at, so if I was you I wouldn't waste any time about climbing onto this bed and then Regal will make you forget about everything you ever did. Come on, Howie boy, let's see what you got, let's see what you can do."

Howard picked up the pillow and tossed it on the bed. "Look, you're just drunk. Why don't you take it easy for a while."

"Drunk? On a lousy half-pint?" Suddenly she let her leg drop to the mattress and gave a cry that was somewhere between a sob and a laugh. "You're afraid he'll catch you, that's it!" Now she began to laugh and roll her head from one side to the other. "Wouldn't that be the thing! You never got caught fucking me, did you? But you see, it don't make any difference now because there's nothing he can do. You see that, can't you, that there's nothing in the world he can do any more?"

"Look," Howard said, "please just take it easy. Do you want me to get a cold washcloth?" He took a step in the direction of the bathroom, then stopped at the foot of the bed.

"And besides . . ." She laughed louder, holding her sides now and still rolling her head back and forth, "you're my husband and you can do anything you want. I heard that in the car and downstairs, but I didn't say anything at the time. You probably have noticed there's not an awful lot of conversation going on between us. I mean, there doesn't seem to be much to talk about. But I believe this should liven things up some. You got a right, you see? Now suppose you caught *him!* That'd be something different. Then what would happen?" She closed her eyes and lay still. Howard remained at the foot of the bed watching her. "It's confusing," Regal said after a while. Her voice was a whisper now. "I'm lucky; I'm a lucky girl; I got two men at the same time. That's doing pretty good in anyone's book. Two for the price of one." She opened her eyes and stared at the ceiling. "But then it's a pretty big price; it's a pretty fucking big price."

Howard walked around to the side of the bed and looked down at her. "What are you talking about? Will you tell me?"

Regal raised herself on her elbows and looked at him. She started to move her mouth, but no words came out. There was a knock at the door. Howard turned but did not move from beside the bed. At the second knock he went over and opened the door.

In the hall was a squat, round-faced boy with red hair hanging over his forehead. When he saw Howard, he took a step backward. "Oops! Sorry, sir, ah was looking for room 2-B. Ah guess ah got the wrong place."

"Ah guess you got the right place!" Regal called from the bed. "Come on in, honey!" The boy looked at Howard again, grinned, and entered. Howard closed the door.

"Ah just happened to run into that fella in Shirley's across the street and . . ."

"I know," Howard said.

The boy rubbed the back of his neck and squinted around the room, everywhere but at the bed. Suddenly he shot his hand out to Howard. "The name's Denton Wiman; Corporal Denton Wiman, that is, from Denton, Texas; that's how ah got my first name."

"My pleasure," Howard said. Regal was flat on her back again, looking at the ceiling.

The soldier cleared his throat. "Are you . . . ah mean, are you just paying a visit up here too, or do you have something to do with it?"

"I've got something to do with it, but I'll be stepping out in the hall for a cigarette now."

"Y'all sure ah'm not interrupting something?"

"No, you go right ahead. I'll be outside."

Regal sat up. "You stay right here! No waiting in the hall and no waiting in the bathroom like you been doing before. You *watch!*"

"Watch?" Denton Wiman said.

"I said I'd be out in the hall and that's where I'll be." Howard opened the door.

"No, you don't understand!" Regal shouted. She scrambled to her feet and stood swaying on the mattress. "You got a right, you got a goddam right. If you can't be the one who's caught, you can be the catcher. You're my *husband!*" She lurched forward and fell to her knees. "We could just see what happened, don't you see?"

"Husband?" said Denton Wiman. "Look, ah tell you what; maybe ah'll just come back a little later." He edged toward the door. "Ah mean ah'll just step out for a while now and then come back. Ah want to say it was real nice meeting y'all and don't worry none about the five dollars." He groped behind him for the doorknob. "Ah mean, ah just got paid so . . ." He was gone.

Howard closed the door. Regal looked at him for a moment, then rolled over on her side and hugged the pillow to her. "It wouldn't have done any harm," she said, her voice muffled against the pillow. "We could've just seen what you would have done if you caught him." She closed her eyes.

"I don't understand," Howard said slowly. "I don't understand what's going on."

It was noon now and through the front window a band of sunlight fell across the floor, catching the bed in its path. The room had become hot and close, and Howard's shirt was damp with sweat. But on the bed Regal was shivering. Howard walked over to her and pulled the spread up over her shoulders.

Margaret awoke at dawn with the feeling that it had only been a few minutes since she had felt Jesse get up. She had lain there listening in the darkness as he dressed, seeing his bent-over silhouette against the window as he pulled on his boots, hearing the creak of the stairs as he made his way down, the slam of the screen door, then the harsh rattle of the truck being started and the steady hum of its engine, which though it grew softer and softer stayed with her until . . . until now? No, it had been hours ago that he had left, for now as she lay on her side and looked out the window the sun was at eye level. The highway was already glazed with sunlight and the faded blue curtains fluttered in the steady desert wind, but there were still long shadows across the bed and the floor, and the room had not yet lost the stillness of night. Margaret sat up and for a moment looked at the faint indentation in Jesse's pillow. As she undid her hair pins she saw that he had left his watch and billfold on the top of the bureau. He had never forgotten them before, and for an instant Margaret felt a quickened concern over the nightly ritual that neither of them spoke of any more, as if each felt a silent acknowledgement was the same as a denial of Jesse's patrols. He would return home each morning about seven, and she would fix him breakfast, and they would not speak. Or, some mornings, he would go directly to the station and she would not see him until evening. At first she had gone through the pretense of asking him whether he had found anyone out there, any motorist who was stranded out there in the middle of the desert; and once at supper he had answered "yes," and had started to describe how he had helped someone with a broken carburetor. But in the middle of a sentence he had just stopped, not with a shrug as though he hadn't felt like explaining it, but had merely gotten up from the table and gone upstairs. She had not asked him since.

When they talked it was of Laura and Howie. At first, when Burt and Laura had moved to Houston, Shaylor had been eager to see the apartment; but after two visits he had seemed to lose interest, and they had made the trip only once in the last eight weeks. Laura was in her fourth month of pregnancy, and Margaret was going alone on the bus to visit her in a few days.

Mostly it was about Howard that Shaylor wanted to talk. In bed before sleep came to her, Margaret would feel his body become tense beside her and would hold off sleep until he had asked, "He *is* all right then you think, Maggie? He'll be back or find a good job some place and settle down. I mean, he won't be just wandering around for the rest of his life? He'll be making something of himself, won't he?" And she would reassure him.

But lately it was he who did the reassuring. "He'll be all right, Maggie. As a matter of fact, the way I figure it, it's the best thing he could've done; it'll get him out of the rut he's been in; I know it will. I mean, every man needs some time out to make some plans. We just don't have to worry about Howie at all is the way I figure it."

The sound of a truck engine reached Margaret; she got up and went to the window. Down the highway an army convoy was approaching slowly. In the lead was a tall-cabbed olive-colored truck with a ribbed canvas back that arched higher than the cab. The truck's yellow headlights glowed weakly in the sunlight. Behind the truck was a column of tanks, their steel treads spilling forward over the blacktop, the long barrels of their turret cannons capped and pointing to the rear. They were followed by ten or twelve low flat-topped vehicles whose smooth iron contours were unbroken except for a thin horizontal slit cut into the frontal plate. At the rear of the convoy was a jeep, its plastic-windowed side panels buckled shut.

All of the vehicles moved at the same speed, the intervals between them never changing, as if they were not moving under their own power but were held together and guided by an unseen link, or were being pulled forward by a signal somewhere in the distance, or were being transported by the highway itself.

Margaret stood watching until the convoy had passed and merged into a single unbroken line in the distance. Then she turned away from the window and on her way to the bathroom stopped to wind Jesse's watch and put his wallet in the top drawer of the bureau.

When she had dressed and made the bed she headed downstairs, but for a moment paused on the top step and looked at Howard's closed bedroom door and at Laura's. There would never have been a right time for them to leave, of course; she knew that—no time when a mother could say, "I'm ready now and if you leave now there will be no feeling of wrenching loss for me because I have expected this and I have prepared for it and I am ready for my children to leave me." No right time, but even so, even knowing that, it *had* been sudden, hadn't it; Howie leaving and then Laura right after? Hadn't it been more sudden than it happens to most mothers? Hadn't it almost been unfair?

Because she knew she would never see Howard again. She would see Laura and would live to see Laura's children grow up and call her grandmother, but she would not live long enough ever to see her son again. He would never come back because he had waited so long before leaving, and the leaving could not be, as Jesse said, a time to think things over before he settled down. It was more than that, it was a flight; and if there were thinking to be done it would come later and would not really be thinking but the recognition that the flight had been a statement, a judgment about his parents, perhaps unrealized at the time, but once made, unalterable. If he returned it could only be as an accuser, as one who has flown and only later has recognized from what he has taken flight. Or he could return wearing a mask and take a part in the lie that for years had been the continuing bond between Jesse and Margaret: Jesse's lie that it had been only the land that had defeated him and that he was not a weak man who when presented with one failure welcomed it and wove it into the fabric of his life so that it became a curtain, in front of which the present and future belonged to a wronged man serving out an unjust sentence, and behind which the world gone by belonged to a man and a dream of happiness which may never really have existed at all; the lie that he was not a selfish man who, like all selfish men, had no sense of self and was forced to rely on someone else—a son or a daughter or a wife—for a reflected image which could be seen if never felt. And Margaret's lie, of course—that she believed him. Howie would not come back. He would not come back at all. And perhaps it would be better.

Slowly, Margaret went down the stairs. We carry our children and they leave us, and we end up carrying our men. But once mustn't there have been promises that she and Jesse had made to themselves and then to each other? Not practical resolutions about the future, or even about the children, but deep commitments that came from youth and then from love. Were they gone now because she and Jesse had not been strong enough to keep them, or were they the wrong promises from the start, ones that couldn't possibly be kept? It made no difference; they were gone and now she could not even remember what they were.

Margaret went into the kitchen and sat down in one of the four chairs pulled up to the table. Her eyes rested for a moment on the corner of the table where the porcelain was worn away. Then she got up quickly, filled a small pan at the sink, and went out to splash water on the live oak tree.

The sun had risen higher than the bug-splattered windshield by the time the panel truck was within ten miles of Hargrett. The truck had covered over a hundred miles since four o'clock that morning, and the metallic whine of the overheated engine was rising in pitch. Bugs were splashed against the headlights too and caught in the grill, their bodies baked into the hot motor cage. Wispy strands of steam seeped out from beneath the silver horse on the hood latch. In back of the cab one of the side panels had slipped from its front groove, and as the truck sped down the highway the board careened out in the wind, then swung back and smacked against the metal brace.

Behind the wheel Shaylor was still wearing the heavy black and white jacket he had put on in the dark bedroom; though his face was red and damp and his eyes bloodshot from looking down the length of the headlight beams and later from squinting into the rising sun, he had neither put down the sun visor nor loosened the jacket. His body had sunk inside the folds of the woolen coat which had ridden up so that the collar in back fanned out almost to the crown of his head and the sleeves hung loosely about his knuckles. Two fingers held a dead cigarette. Although the sunlight that came in the side window glanced off his face, the deep lines it accentuated and his mottled growth of overnight beard and the puffiness about his eyes made his face seem as if it had not yet come out of the night. Not only his face but his whole body, rigid and diminished inside the jacket, seemed not a part of the new glaring day at all but of the early morning hours of darkness, as if the journey had long since gone beyond any fixed relation to a point of departure or point of termination and in doing so had become caught in time.

But outside the day grew. The truck passed through Hooten Junction. In a small wheat field a man and boy primed the engine of a thresher. Two school girls were sitting on an orange crate in front of a gas station, their lunch boxes and books lined up neatly beside them. And the armored procession continued down the highway, the intervals between the vehicles remaining the same.

There was a smell of cattle you couldn't lose. When you brought 'em down to bind their legs on a branding day you'd dig your shoulder into the base of the little one's neck; and when you got him down you'd hold him till the ropes were tight and your cheek up hard against the flat muscle of the fella's neck, and your nostrils would fill up with the thick warm smell of hide and bristle. At the end of the day your cheek would be slick with oil and scratched red from the bristle, and your mouth would be fuzzy with hair, and your body alive with the feel and the smell of cattle.

You never really lost it any more than you lost the jump in your belly when it was your own brand the iron was burning into their flanks. And that's why it was so simple now that the only question was why it had taken him so long to make his move. He could get the money; that wouldn't be any problem. Jack Dwyer at the bank would let him have it on loan for a year or so until things started rolling. Or even Boyd—he must have tucked something away over the years from the station. Anyway, getting it wouldn't be a problem; there were a lot of people around town who hadn't forgotten that when it came to having an eye for cattle you'd have to put Jesse Shaylor pretty far up near the top of the list. They wouldn't think it was just the talk of an old man.

Of course, nobody in his right mind would ever think of starting up a ranch around Hargrett where there wasn't enough good grassland to feed a Mexican mule or enough water to wet down the roof of a hen's mouth. No, they'd have to hightail it out of Hargrett, and that'd be part of it, part of making the start. He knew places . . . up farther north near Kilburn or San Pedro Springs or even Creighton. Wouldn't it be something to go back to Creighton where they started? The grass was good now with the new dam they built way up on the Loop River—the same river that for him had flowed only dust and stones. And there might even be a couple of old-timers still there who'd stake him to a few head and a couple of dozen acres, till he got things rolling.

It'd be something, but maybe there were other places even better. It'd been a long time since he'd done any scouting around, and maybe Howie had come across some places while he'd been on the road. Of course, he'd have to check them out himself. You had to know just the kind of spread that would work, but still, if the boy. . . . Because Howie would be a part of it, and that was something that should have been clear as daylight to him a long time ago—that Howie was just waiting for him to say the word, and that instead of trying to give him lectures about how he should be out looking for a job he should have been looking around *with* him so they could make the start together. Hell, it was all so damn clear now; starting out small like they'd have to, it'd just *need* two men at first; a two-man operation—Howie and him. And then by the time they got bigger, maybe in a year or two, and needed to take on some more hands, he'd already have had enough time to teach Howie all he needed to know to run the whole spread by himself. Then he could sit back and watch; maybe giving some advice now and then about picking out the breeders or when to buy and sell, but mostly he'd be taking a back seat. And that's the way it ought to be, the father teaching the son all the tricks and the son gradually taking over from the father. That's the way it would be.

He had the brains, Howie; you couldn't take that away from him no matter what else. It was just that he needed a little help, a little shove in the right direction. And goddam! If it isn't the father that gives him the help, who is it?

Outside the wind swept twigs and snarls of tumbleweed across the highway. The oil-black telegraph poles were slick with sunlight now. The early morning green had been baked out of the desert scrub, and three miles in front of the truck the sun had spread a dull glaze across the flat olive roofs of the squat rectangular vehicles in the armored procession.

Shaylor's hands loosened on the wheel. The dead cigarette dropped between his knees. As if it would ever work out. As if there was even a chance in a million that Howie'd give a damn about being partners and making a new start. No, if Howie did anything more than shrug it'd just be to make some excuse, that he had to take care of some other things first or that it all sounded like a good idea but maybe he ought to get another partner instead, somebody who knew something about the cattle business. Or maybe he would agree, pretend to be enthusiastic, pretend he didn't think it was all talk and wouldn't ever amount to anything else.

And Maggie, she'd do the same thing as Howie, only a little different. She'd nod her head, pretending she believed in his plans and asking him all the right questions, only the ones that any fool could answer easy, always staying on the surface and not knowing that he knew she was treating him like a goddam baby that had to be petted and nursed along on a tit and wrapped up in a blanket so it wouldn't get into any trouble. It had been that way for a long time. Every evening: "How's things at the station today, Jess?" As if things were ever any different when all you did every day was fill up somebody's gas tank or fix a flat or drain a crank case or clean up the grease rack or do whatever Boyd told you to do—things that even a goddam half-wit like the Pendleton kid could do with one arm behind his back. "How's things at the station?" Maybe it was her way of getting back at him. As if he wanted it to end up this way, with her wearing that quiet understanding face that turned sad when she thought he wasn't looking at her. Well, it was just too damn bad, too bad if he hadn't lived up to . . . oh, Maggie! Maggie! Maggie!

And of course it *was* just all talk. Howie would listen and Maggie would listen, but they were right not to pay any real attention because he wasn't even really paying any attention himself. It was just a make-believe dream of an old man to make up for the real dreams that a younger man didn't have the guts to hold onto.

Shaylor's hands tightened on the steering wheel. His foot pressed down on the accelerator. Oh, but Maggie, they were good dreams! Remember how we used to lie awake at night and talk about how it'd be when the ranch was doing well enough to run itself; how we were going to get a big car and every weekend zip up to Houston or Dallas and stay in a fancy hotel with a swimming pool and waiters who brought us our breakfast in bed. We were going to go dancing till after midnight. And how every year we were going to take maybe a month's vacation—just you and me without the kids—and go to New York or even Europe if we felt like it. It was going to be Maggie in a Paris hat!

The truck would do sixty; it wouldn't do sixty-five.

Yeah, well, they're better off out of it—Laura with her insurance boy and even Howie running away from it. Only you, Maggie. You would too, you see; you'd be better off . . . Well, it's too bad you still gotta be in it because you'd be better off. You see what I mean? You see what I'm saying? Better off, better than still in it, and it's too bad that you gotta be and better to be left. You see . . . Yeah, well, I can still hang on, you see; oh, I could always . . . I could always ride; nobody said there was anybody rides better than me. You dig your heels in like this and you hang on and oh, it'll try to shake you; it'll shake and back around under you so's you think it'll throw you any minute, but you dig in and you're riding faster than you ever thought you could; and then, oh yeah, when you see 'em coming at you like this what you gotta do is . . . coming at you big and mean and they mean business because you can see their eyes catching the sunlight, big eyes yellow and alive, but there's only one way to do it and that's ride right into 'em and then watch 'em scatter . . . if you can hang on, that's the only thing, until you run right into 'em dead center and . . . and, why, remember when I got 'em that morning with the rig and it took your breath away? I'd brushed 'em and curried 'em until they was like . . . silver! They was silver horses and I got one now! I'm riding a silver horse and I'm riding it 'cause you got to, right into the center of 'em, and then watch 'em scatter when they know you're hanging on. Watch 'em! Watch 'em! Riding in on a silver horse!

It was Burt who broke the ten-minute silence. "For Christ's sake, Laurie, you don't have to carry on like a goddam hound dog. I'm not trying to force you into anything. You didn't like any of the other places, *any* of them that we've seen, so all we're doing is going to look at another one just in case you might happen to think it isn't so bad. I mean, it's just possible that we might be in a hell of a lot better shape if we move *before* the baby comes than if we wait until after." Burt stopped for a red light, then turned left on Parkhurst. Beside him Laura smoked a cigarette. She was wearing a pale-blue maternity smock, white ankle socks and black loafers. She had tied an orange bandana about her head, but a few long strands of hair fell over her face. She sat with her knees apart, one hand held against her swollen stomach.

Burt sighed and reached over to touch her thigh. "I apologize; I didn't mean to sound so damn irritated. It's been pretty rough for you; I know that. I mean, I know it's going to take a long time for you to get over your father and there's nothing anybody can say that'll make it any easier. And then on top of that with the baby coming soon . . . Well, I had no right to snap at you. I apologize."

Laura smiled and nodded without looking at him. The cigarette had burned down to a half inch, and smoke filtered up between her fingers. She threw the butt out the window.

Burt adjusted the brim of his fedora. "But the thing is, you were kind of acting the same way *before* he died. Every time we went out to look at a place I got the feeling you didn't really care anything about getting a house of our own and were even holding some kind of a grudge against *me,* as if, like I said before, I was trying to force you into something against your will. I mean, it was our *plan,* Laurie; it was! We talked all about it —that after we started having a family we'd move into a place of our own. I know you like the apartment and we haven't been there long, but it was only temporary; you knew that. And maybe some of these places we looked at weren't all that great, but damn, I don't believe you even gave 'em a chance, Laurie. Before we even walked into a place you had your mind set that you weren't going to like it even if it'd been a palace. I don't believe you'd have noticed if it *was* a palace anyway, because you don't really look at anything even when we get inside. I don't believe I'm being all that unreasonable to expect you to take at least *some* interest. I mean, most people look forward to having a home of their own, and a lot of people dream about it for years but can't ever afford it. The way I figure it we're pretty damn lucky. I'm willing to bet there's not an awful lot of couples going house hunting after they've only been married five months, and you can bet also that there'll be plenty of eyes opening wide back in Hargrett when the word gets around that Mr. and Mrs. Burt Curtis have acquired a private home in Houston. We're pretty damn lucky! Sure, we'll have to make payments every month and maybe it would've been nice to have bought that plot of land I was talking about a while back, but the way I figure it there's a lot of people who wouldn't mind being in the shape we are." Burt cleared his throat. "I'm not exactly a slouch when it comes to selling insurance, you know; and, as a matter of fact, owning your own house can be a real help to business. Sure, you can have a prospect and his wife over to your apartment, but it's not the same thing as inviting them over for some nice tall drinks and a barbecue in your own back yard—not by any stretch of the imagination." They passed a warehouse. Two boys sat on the edge of the empty loading platform eating ice-cream cones. "You know what else helps, Laurie? Having a wife who takes some pride in making the home a place people will enjoy visiting." Burt let his hand rest on Laura's knee for a moment. "I'm not talking about right now; you know that, don't you? Because don't think I don't have a pretty good idea of the way you're feeling. I do, Laurie, and the only thing I wish is there was something I could do to make you feel real better in a hurry. But I don't believe there's anything wrong in talking about the future. You know, this baby's going to make a real difference. I mean, it would have anyway, but especially now, and especially to you. You know what was going through my mind a couple of minutes back? I was thinking that the baby's going to not only take your mind off your father some, but, well . . . I don't mean this the way it sounds, but it's almost that, if your father had to die now, it makes it even more right that we should be having the baby. Not that I'm saying the baby is going to take the place of your father; nothing could do that. But it's like when one life is over it's time for another one to begin. Do you see what I mean?"

Laura pressed the dashboard lighter and waited until it had popped out and she had lit her cigarette before she answered him. "Yes, I see what you mean."

"And you know he'd be pretty proud of you if he could see you in your own house serving dinner to friends or giving a party or maybe having a few people over in the evening to watch television. You see, that's why I was beginning to get a little worried when you didn't even give any of these places we looked at a fair chance. I'm not saying that I was all set to buy at any time, but still, if I *had* been interested, the way you were acting would've kind of put a crimp in things; you got to admit that, Laurie." Burt tapped the steering wheel. "Well, never mind, we're doing all right and I don't blame you for being choosey. We're going to have a *good* place, right? Remember how we were talking before we got married? Well, that still goes. We're going to do things right. We're going to have a good old place."

Had it been at Mary Jean Cameron's, the day three of them ate a whole watermelon? Yes, out in the back yard; Mary Jean, Buddy Andruss and herself, laughing and talking and stuffing themselves, pointing at each other as the juice ran down their chins and onto their clothing. And each one knowing they would be sick unless they stopped, but together unable to stop until all of the red juicy melon had been eaten down to the rind. And then, stomachs bloated and aching, they had collapsed on the lawn and tried not to laugh and, of course, had laughed all the more. And had it really only been last May and not years ago? Waiting between one life that was over and another that had not yet begun. But Burt had been talking of her father and the baby. She hardly ever thought about her father. No, that wasn't it; she tried to think of him, tried to focus the general awareness that something had happened into a sharp immediate feeling that something had happened to *him* which affected her. There was the horror of the accident, the image of the devastated truck and the possibility of pain, but even the actual event could be conjured up only so many times before time and repetition dulled the initial horror. Maybe later there would be something more, a chain of thoughts or feelings that could be linked about the event to give it a place and a perspective in her own life. But her father had been dying for a long time; the four of them knew that, and the act of death had not really introduced anything new but only left her unsure of how she should react to it. It was herself she thought of at Burt's words, and apart from anything else it was herself whom she felt to be between a life ended and one not yet begun. She had left Hargrett because if she stayed she would be waiting like everyone else, until the expectation became the thing itself. Except for her father, who had known all along what he was waiting for. And now that she had left . . . Now it was not fair to Burt, the man she had chosen to take her away, to hold herself apart from him and from his child. For if her marriage and the leaving and now the child inside her had not yet filled the emptiness of the life she had wished ended, they would; they would soon. Because she *did* care about her husband, and his plans and dreams were hers too. She did care.

Burt slowed the car as they drove under the large Billy Jo Webber Garden Estates banner stretched between two telephone poles. Ahead of them a half-dozen streets radiated out from a huge traffic circle with a green-cement island in its center. The circle was on a slight rise, and below on the other side silver aerials caught the noon sun and splintered it above the tops of hundreds of Easter-colored houses; spilling over the rusty earth to the horizon, the houses sparkled in the sun as if they had sucked their blues and greens, yellows and pinks from the now colorless sky. At first the houses seemed merely to have been scattered across the basin like an enormous handful of colored dice; but as Burt followed the Model Homes arrow the car descended into a labyrinth of streets scraped into the earth but not yet paved, no street continuing for more than two hundred yards before it spliced into the new streets. Ten houses lined each side of every street. No color repeated itself until four houses later; each third house had its carport on the left rather than right side; picture windows alternated from left to right too, but every front sidewalk split the same size rectangular lawn of raked dirt. On some houses the front steps faced the street directly, on others they were built into the side of a small foyer. The intersections were marked by red fire hydrants impaled a foot above the ground on black iron shafts.

Burt, still following arrows, made a right turn. Houses lined only one side of the new street; on the other side was a row of shallow rectangular pits, each lined with steel webbing. In back of them the neck and silver-toothed jaw of an orange steam shovel hovered over a squat bulldozer whose blade was half buried in a pile of loose soil.

They made a left turn into a street where a row of three houses stood alone in the middle of the block. The first house was light blue with a white panel extending across it as high as the base of the windows; the second was pink with a yellow panel, and the third white with a light blue panel. Stretched tight across each lawn on both sides of the front walk and fastened at the corners with stakes was a green canvas tarpaulin.

Burt pulled up in front of the first house, looked at Laura for a moment, then switched off the engine. He got out and came around to help her. A thin layer of dust had settled on the tarpaulin; the wind was blowing it around in small whirlpools as they went up the walk.

The front door was open; somewhere inside a television set was on. Burt hesitated at the door for a few seconds, then stepped in, Laura following.

They were in the living room. A couch and three chairs in the front of the room were covered with clear plastic slipcovers. The floor was maroon linoleum shot with strands of white. On it were two fluffy yellow throw rugs. A black-and-gold tree lamp stood in one corner. The television set was in another. Standing in front of the set was a man about thirty-five, thin with black hair sleeked straight back from his forehead. He stood with one hand on his hip, the other hooked into his belt. He was wearing a white shirt with a light blue string tie, blue pants, and white slippers. A minute went by before he looked away from the set and saw Burt and Laura in the doorway.

"Oh, hi!" He reached over and turned down the volume, then stared at them for a second, ran a hand over his hair, and wet his lips. "I mean, oh hello there! I'm Lamar Perkins. I'm so glad that you happened to be in our community this afternoon and decided to drop in for a visit." While he was talking his eyes strayed back to the television set. On the screen, a girl on the shoulders of a water-skier was holding a tray of beer bottles. "Coca-Cola!" Lamar Perkins said loudly. "I bet you folks wouldn't mind one about now. I wouldn't be surprised if there's some out in the kitchen. Why don't I go and rustle up some." He looked at the set for another ten seconds, smoothed back his hair again, then disappeared around a back corner of the living room. Perkins returned with two cokes. Burt and Laura moved in closer to the television set. On the screen now, a cartoon cowboy lassoed a can of soup.

"Here it is; nice and cold too."

"None for me, thank you," Laura said.

"What?" He handed a Coke to Burt. "You mean you don't want any?" He stared at her. "Oh, oh, I see. Yes." He took a step backward. "Well . . ." he cleared his throat. "We call this model the Coronet. The living room is a full eighteen by twelve feet; more than enough room, as you can see, for a dining area in the back that saves unneeded steps from kitchen to table. That's only one small example of . . ." He looked behind him for a place to set the Coke bottle, then put it on top of the television set, in front of which the three of them now formed a semicircle. On the screen a small boy was brushing his teeth. ". . . one small example of the comfort-consciousness which went into the design of this particular model, many other features of which you will discover as we explore other parts of the model. You see, one of the reasons we think this house speaks for itself is because long before we would even allow folks like you to see it, something very unusual took place." Perkins' eyes flicked across the set. "This model was *family tested.*" He smoothed the front of his shirt and folded his arms. "I think you folks might be interested in just what I mean when I say *family tested.* The term is exclusive with Billy Jo Webber Garden Estates, by the way, for the simple reason that Mr. Webber himself created the only method that exists of family testing a home. Long before the first shovelful of dirt was broken on the estates, the Coronet had passed the test." Perkins rubbed his hands together. "Here's how it worked; we built a Coronet—exactly like this one—in another part of town and moved an average family of four and all their belongings in for one month. Now all of them lived their average lives; the husband went to his office every day as usual; the wife did her usual chores; the youngsters went to their school. At night they'd all have their supper, watch TV just like anybody. Only one thing different; we gave each of them—youngsters included—a notebook in which we asked them to jot down, every night, anything they especially *liked* or *disliked* about the Coronet on that particular day. Now you see *every day* they were doing that. And we told them, don't worry about repeating yourself from day to day because that's part of it. In other words, we didn't want them to feel they had to come up with something different each time—just whatever came into their heads."

Burt looked at Laura who had sat down on the couch and was staring at the TV screen. "You mean like a diary?"

"That's right," Perkins said, "a diary of the Coronet. Well . . ." He pulled a hair from his ear and examined it a moment. "For the first two weeks the notebooks were filled with things we expected. For instance, the husband liked the width of the carport—you probably noticed that it's a full nine feet wide. And the wife . . . well, when you take a look at the kitchen a little bit later you'll understand why *she* didn't have any trouble finding things to jot down each night." Perkins smiled for an instant. "But don't think I'm going to try to tell you there weren't things that they *didn't* like at first. For instance, one of the youngsters wrote that there was no place to *hide* when he didn't want anybody to find him. And once the husband put down that he missed having to go upstairs to a bedroom. I've got a photostat of the notebooks, by the way, if you'd like to look at them; they make interesting reading."

"Did you make any changes on the basis of them?" Burt asked.

Perkins sliced the air with his hand. "Ah, that's the most interesting aspect of all. As I said earlier, the entire family wrote something in their notebooks every night for the *first two weeks.* Then, gradually, the jottings began to taper off until finally, the last week . . . nothing. You know what that meant, don't you?" He drove his fist into his palm. "It meant that they were no longer thinking of the Coronet as a thing to be evaluated by good and bad points—plusses and minuses, if you would. They had accepted it as a home—*their* home." He folded his arms and looked at Laura, then Burt, then bowed his head slightly. "When we saw the same pattern in each of the notebooks we knew we had passed the family test."

Burt carefully set his Coca-Cola bottle down next to the other one. "Well, that sounds like a real original approach. Did you do the same thing with the houses next door?"

Perkins raised his head. "I'm afraid I wouldn't know about the models next door. I'm sure they're quite nice." He put his hands behind his back and walked in a small circle. "Well, you've already seen the living room now. It's a full twelve by eighteen, by the way, plenty of room in the rear for a dining area with a family-size table, and only a few steps from the kitchen of course. The flooring comes in a choice of fifteen color combinations, and of course we guarantee it for a full two years. What I think might be a good idea now is for you to see the rest of the home from bottom to top, not from top to bottom; a little twist there, but I always think it's best to start with the basics. So why don't we take a look at the cellar first so you can get a look at your furnace and your hot water heater and the laundry room where there's plenty of space for your washer and dryer." Perkins smiled at Laura. "Of course, if you don't feel like climbing up and down stairs right now, ma'am, I'm sure your husband will be able to fill you in on everything down there." He chuckled. "That is, if you trust his report."

Laura smiled back from the couch. "Thank you; maybe I *will* wait here for now."

"Yeah, that's right," Burt said. "I don't believe there's much point in you having to look at the basement. You just take it easy for a while and maybe mosey around up here by yourself if you feel like it. I'll be right back." He and Perkins went out through the alcove, and a moment later Laura heard them going down the basement steps. The smile was still on her face.

She tried to stop smiling because her cheeks and the corners of her eyes were beginning to ache and because . . . "Someday you're going to freeze like that," Howie would say when she made a face at him. Someday to be frozen. If it happened would it begin like this, in her stomach with a circle of ice that spread throughout her body to her arms and legs until she was unable to move, until her body became so cold and brittle that she was afraid if she tried to move even slightly, even breathed, she would splinter and crack into a thousand pieces? She sat there, and it didn't make any difference whether she held her breath or not because there was something pressing in on her now that enveloped her body and compressed it until suddenly the circle of ice burst in her stomach and not ice but hot liquid was forced up through her chest to her throat. Laura choked and pushed herself up from the couch. She ran across the linoleum floor to the front steps, and there, bent over the cast iron railing, she closed her eyes and a moment later heard the sour liquid spattering on the canvas lawn.

She was dizzy. Her smock was soaked with sweat. She

steadied herself on the railing for a moment, then went back into the house and walked slowly through the living room and into the kitchen. She tried the cold water tap, but the knob turned loosely and nothing came out. She stood there for a moment with her hand on the knob, hearing the men's voices in the cellar. She sat down at the small linoleum-topped table in one corner and let her fingers trail along the metal strip that bordered its edge. Then she sat up straight. It was with her now, the feeling that she had either not been able or had not wanted to recognize. But it had come to her now so quickly and strongly that she grabbed onto the sides of the table. *I wanted him to die. That's what we were waiting for. I* wanted that most of all. We all wanted his death but couldn't ever admit it, and maybe that's why Howie left—because finally he couldn't stand the waiting any more. Or maybe for him it didn't make any difference whether Papa lived or died. But it did for me. I couldn't even leave; I couldn't do it by myself while he was alive. I couldn't stand the waiting either, but now it's over and now shouldn't there be beginning a kind of freedom? Isn't that what I was waiting for—a kind of freedom? Her eyes wandered over the stainless-steel windowed oven built flush into the laminated pine-paneled wall. Its row of control buttons were the same pink as the floor, the table top, the sink counter, and the refrigerator which stood in its own rectangular nook in the wall. The stainless-steel vault beneath the sink was open wide enough to reveal the white dishwashing racks. Through the small window above the sink she could see a yellow bulldozer.

They were coming up the stairs now. Laura stood up and immediately felt the sharp pain of the new life inside her. She stood in the middle of the room with her back to the cellar stairs and her eyes closed, and she pressed down hard on her stomach, digging her fingers into her bloated flesh under the smock as if to stop the movement of that new life.

They were at the top of the stairs. She could hear Burt breathing heavily.

"Well, what do you think, Laurie?"

She opened her eyes; the sun made them water. "I like it."

"Sure you do," Lamar Perkins said.

At midnight on a bench in the waiting room of the Bartonsville Greyhound terminal a milky-skinned elderly woman in a lavender coat and black straw hat was reading a copy of the *Digest.* A soldier dozed beside her, his cap pulled down to shield his eyes from the fluorescent lights, his feet propped up on his duffle bag. Across the aisle from them a thin girl with russet curls piled on top of her head took a kerchief from the drawstring canvas bag next to her. She folded it on her lap into a triangle, laid it carefully over her hair, and tied the ends in a bow under her chin. Then she reached into the bag for a cigarette, lit it, crossed her legs, and adjusted her skirt over her knees.

Crow, leaning against the Dr. Pepper machine, had been watching her for ten minutes. What he could do was just bring her a soda and sit down next to her. He looked over at the soldier and felt in his lefthand pocket for change. Or he could just stroll by her and say something like, "You think it's ever going to show up?" Then if she answered him or smiled he could follow that remark up quick with something else; and if she didn't say anything or make any kind of a sign to him he could just keep on walking, and nobody would know the difference. He looked around the station. In back a Mexican boy was sweeping out the ticket seller's cage. Out in front, in the red glow of the neon sign, two men lounged against a Ford pick-up truck.

Crow watched the girl step on her cigarette. She was wearing a gold anklet. Christ! There had been that doll on the bus a few days ago. As soon as he got on he knew she was giving him the eye; you could tell. The only trouble was, it was a little tough to handle because there were only about three or four people on the whole goddam bus, so what could he do at first except take the seat right behind her? And that was working out perfect too, because through the crack between the seats he could see she was beginning to sigh and twist around into different positions, and then . . . goddam son of a bitch! The next station was Waco, and about twenty people got on; and of course this fat bastard traveling-salesman-looking guy sits down next to her, and only a few minutes after they pull out of Waco he sees the back of their heads already sinking down lower in the seats. For the next two hundred fifty miles he's got to sit there next to some prune-faced old bitch, knowing every move that's going on in front of him, and knowing the doll would have wanted it to be him up there a million times more than the fat bastard salesman.

The red-haired girl was lighting another cigarette. That would be another way—to walk over and ask her for a smoke. Well, shit! That was about the oldest routine in the world, and besides, she might take him for a bum. No, the best way was with the sodas, nice and friendly and with no harm intended. "Figured you might be getting a little dry about now."

Crow got two dimes out of his pocket and slipped one into the machine. A paper cup dropped down and two parallel streams of clear and brown liquid hissed into it. He put the other dime in. The soda was warm, and the plastic-coated cups wiggled in his hands. He poured a little soda of each into the drain and turned around just in time to see a tall man in a Stetson come through the front door of the terminal. He walked directly over to the girl. Without speaking, he picked up her drawstring bag. She got up and followed him out of the station.

Crow stood there holding the cups. "Watch it, grandma," he said under his breath to the woman in the lavender coat who had put down her *Digest* to look at him. "Unless you want a snootful of this before you know what hit you." He looked down at his pants at the bulge that was partly covered by his leather jacket. "Or maybe there's something else you'd like a taste of." The Mexican boy was sweeping the middle aisle now. He too looked over at Crow. Crow leaned casually against the soda machine, drank one cupful of warm Dr. Pepper, then the other. He dropped the cups into a wire trash basket and headed for the men's room.

Inside, he bolted the door and took the revolver from his pants. He stood there a moment facing the door, then whirled around, dropped to one knee and clicked the trigger at the wall. There'd be some people who'd find out it didn't pay to pull a fast one. He got up and examined the gun. It was an army .45, and he'd swapped for it with twenty gallons of motor oil he'd buried a year ago near the railroad tracks in Hargrett. He'd been on the road a month now, hitchhiking and using buses, and he'd catch up with them pretty soon. There weren't that many places they'd be heading for; mostly soldier towns, and they'd be trying to get there on payday weekends. Just a couple of days ago in Killeen that fellow had recognized their descriptions. He'd catch up with them pretty soon.

Crow shoved the revolver back into his pants, smoothed the jacket down over it and went out into the waiting room. The old lady was looking at him again. He stuck out his tongue. It was a good feeling to know he could blow off the top of her head if he wanted to.

Part Three

IN DECEMBER the sun is a hard white ball sitting up there above the driving desert wind that sweeps the land bare. It is a sun that can still set the road to shaking at noon and give you a fair burn if you're out under it for any length of time, but mostly it's not the sun that's on your mind this time of year. In December it's the wind that works hard. Try walking head-on into it along the edge of the highway or on a rise of open land. Five minutes and the skin on your forehead is stretched so tight you think it's going to split. What begins as a tickle in your ears becomes a roar and then a numbing ache, as if someone was shooting ice-water into your eardrums. And all this time you're walking bent over with your head tucked into your chest and your eyes squinted half shut. Walk straight-up and the wind will blind you with tears, and then dust that gets up under your lids and scratches your eyeballs red.

You'll feel it if you're driving too. Coming down the highway in the cab of a semi, you'll know it when a gust of wind smacks up against your trailer; and it won't make any difference whether you're hauling feather mattresses or cement blocks. You'll hear the hitch squeaking behind you and feel the trailer tugging to one side, and, though it's crazy even to think it could happen on a dry straightaway with a full load, you'll shoot a look into the side view mirror to make sure the trailer's not jackknifing up to smack you off the road.

In a car you really feel it. Sometimes you've got to use the steering wheel like a rudder; and if you forget to work it, or if you take your eyes from the road too long, you find you're heading toward the edge. And even if you're careful the sudden gusts can still wrench the wheel out of your hands.

It was close to midnight, and Howard was driving. Hubble slept next to him, his head resting against the side window. Regal was stretched out flat on the back seat. As it had for months, the smell of liquor permeated the car, but it had been a long time since Hubble had said anything about Regal's drinking or had even seemed to care where she got her bottles. It was part of the change that Howard had sensed in both Hubble and Regal. Regal no longer got drunk; she was never really sober. In her half-somnambulent world there was no more crying, no more hysterical outbursts, no more baiting Howard. She did what she was told, and she did it automatically, without emotion. But there was something else about her that either had not been there before or had not been apparent to Howard. He sensed it now, behind her docility. Some small part of herself Regal was keeping in reserve; some part of her being had not yet become benumbed by the nightly acts committed on her body.

Maybe Hubble hadn't changed. You couldn't really tell because when could you ever get enough insight into him to judge? It was still Hubble's show, and nobody was going to argue about that. If there was going to be any trouble, he was going to be on both ends—starting it and finishing it. But there was never any trouble. They drove their circuit from Cullman to San Antonio to Waco to Killeen, up to Wichita Falls and back, with a dozen small towns in between; and they had driven it maybe ten times in six months, never staying in a town more than one night. There wasn't any trouble, and maybe it was because every town, big or small, was the same and had been rehearsed a hundred times. But maybe also it was because a night clerk waiting in a calendared cubicle under a curl of flypaper saw in the three faces something so far removed from the familiar visitations of round-shouldered salesmen and milky old women that it seemed better to let it have its own way, better to leave it alone. So, although Hubble still gave the orders, there were few orders to give. Each of the three of them played his role—in the car, in a café jammed with soldiers, behind the guarded door of a walk-up hotel room.

And if sometimes, at midnight on a deserted highway, or looking out a hotel window at a courthouse which could have been the same one he had stared at the night before, Howard might ask himself why he was here, why he stayed; most of the time it was too much of an effort to come up with an answer that had anything to do with the world he had left; and that was an answer in itself. He was here because they had forty-five miles to go before they got to the next town. He was here because if Hubble got at least six stooges to come up to the room they would have enough money to get through the next day. And once in a while, when he could focus in on that other world, he would know that he was here because there was no other place to be; that all the talk in Hargrett of freedom, his talk, had been a lie; that the parts they had all acted out there—of a father or a son or a husband or wife—were all lies. Freedom was gone from them because they were all caught in the isolation of promises which they themselves had either broken or never awakened to, caught in the self-hatred and loneliness which made impossible either a beginning or a return of love and truth. And if it had happened to his father and to all the men of Hargrett, why should it be different for him? If they had started out wanting something and had lost everything, why should he, who did not even know what he wanted, find in a dream or a plan anything more than a shadow world, the world they had found in Hargrett where they were haunted by their own shadows.

The pimp and the prostitute cast no shadows; and if between Hubble and Regal there was no acknowledgement of each other's existence beyond the animal knowledge that each played a part in the survival of both, wasn't it, if anything, better than what went on in Hargrett? Was there open acknowledgement between his mother and father of what their lives had become?

Did Laura admit, even to herself, why she would marry Burt Curtis? Wasn't the only difference that for Hubble and Regal the surface of their lives was all, and perhaps all they had ever had, while for his father the surface was only a cover for the lies and disappointment underneath? The difference was that Hubble had taken the shortcut. And maybe he had saved a lot of trouble.

So Howard was here because he was at the wheel of the Hudson with the pimp next to him and the prostitute in back, and he was here because there was no place else to be. And for one more reason—because he could not completely believe his own thoughts. He was waiting for something to happen. He had waited in Hargrett, and nothing had happened. But, although Hubble had told him he was only fooling himself if he thought anything was ever coming his way, Regal had called him a witness. A witness to what? He wanted to know.

They had driven for six hours straight and were on the outskirts of Weldon now. There was a roadhouse ahead. "You want to stop for something to eat?" Howard asked. Hubble made no answer. Howard pulled the Hudson into the parking lot and switched off the engine.

"What's the matter?" Hubble was sitting up. He straightened the leather cap.

"Nothing's the matter. I'm hungry." Howard got out of the car and went up the front steps of the roadhouse. The throb of the juke box came through the door.

On the other side of the door was a dimly lit cement room about fifty feet square. The bar was along one wall; round-topped tables lined the adjacent two and a bandstand was against the wall opposite. In the center of the ceiling hung a large metal chandelier which turned slowly and sent thin shafts of colored light around the room. Howard sat down at a table. A half-dozen men were at the bar, bottles of beer in front of them. A soldier was studying the juke box.

When the door opened again the men turned to look. Hubble stood in the doorway a moment, then came in. Behind him

Regal walked unsteadily, hugging a sweater about her shoulders. They sat down at Howard's table, and the men at the bar turned back to their bottles.

"Gimme a cigarette," Hubble said. Howard pushed the pack across the table. Hubble leaned back and looked around the room. "This place stinks."

Howard shrugged. "Well, I don't give much of a damn as long as I get something to eat."

Hubble blew a stream of smoke across the table. "Watch it, sonny; watch it." Regal laughed.

A bulky woman in her sixties was standing next to the table. She had on a black sateen dress and a white vinyl apron. "Chef's gone. I can give you folks ham sandwiches if you want."

Hubble and Howard nodded. Regal looked up. "I'll have a whisky, please. You can make it a double, and you don't have to bother about bringing water with it." She rested her chin in her hands.

The waitress fingered the pencil stuck in her hair. "You're in Texas now, ma'am. We sell beer across the counter, and we can give you a set-up if you got your bottle with you, but that's all we can do for you. I know there's lots of places that'll break the law for a dollar and sneak you a mixed drink in a coffee mug, or maybe cover it up by bringing you a ginger ale bottle along with your glass so people'll think you're just having ginger ale and nothing else; but we don't trifle with the law here. You gotta be careful when you run a café in a soldier town. All you gotta do is get caught just once and . . ."

"Ham sandwiches," Hubble said. "Bring three of 'em."

The waitress plunked the pencil out of her hair and wrote down the order on her pad. "Y'all want three bottles of beer along with that?"

"You know what we want, ma'am?" Howard said slowly. "We want three ham sandwiches." The waitress looked at Regal and left.

Hubble was staring at Howard's watch. It was twelve-thirty.

"All right, here's what we do; we check into the hotel tonight and we start working at two o'clock tomorrow afternoon, and we get out of town by seven tomorrow night." Regal was playing with the colored shafts of light that fanned across the table.

"It's up to you," Howard said, "but if this is a payday weekend like you said, it seems to me there'll be a lot more soldiers in town later at night than in the afternoon."

Hubble spread his hands flat on the table. "You hear anybody ask you for your ideas? You hear somebody say it's time for you to start running things? Yeah, there'll be more soldiers in town at night, and there'll be more drunks and M. P.'s and state cops too. All we need is just one drunk making noise . . ."

He broke off speaking because the soldier who had been standing at the juke box was in front of the table now. He stood with his hands at his sides, as straight as if he had been called to attention. He was about nineteen. His hair was clipped so short that even in the dim light you could see his scalp and the bunching of muscles at his temples.

When the soldier spoke it was with the polite voice of a Southerner. "Excuse me, sir." He bowed to both Hubble and Howard. "But I just wonder if I might have a dance with the lady. I'm not trying to pull anything wise, but I been sitting around this place all night, having a couple of beers and listening to some music; now it's about time I got to be getting back to the camp, and I sure would appreciate one dance—that is, if it's all right with y'all and if the lady feels like dancing." Neither Hubble nor Howard spoke. The soldier remained at attention.

Then, slowly, Regal got to her feet and smoothed her skirt. The soldier hesitated a moment, then offered his arm. They walked to the center of the room.

They began to dance, and the men at the bar shifted on their stools to watch. They began to dance in a small circle, then moved out from beneath the chandelier and slowly danced around the room. They danced in and out of the colored lights.

Regal's eyes were closed; the soldier's hand on her waist guided her. Over the music you could hear their shoes scraping the cement floor. Regal's sweater slipped from her shoulders, but no one made a move to pick it up. No one moved in the room but Regal and the soldier. The waitress stood in the kitchen doorway with the tray of sandwiches. The bartender, his arms resting on the cash register, watched over the heads of the men at the bar. Across the room at the round white table, Hubble and Howard watched.

Regal and the soldier turned, dipped, and for an instant it seemed that Regal would fall. But the soldier caught her, and now they circled the room against the movement of the lights, dancing through a dark pool with multi-colored waves washing over them. Regal, in her white dress with her hair swirling about her shoulders, was diaphanous.

Then Hubble got to his feet. He made no move toward the dance floor, but stood with one hand resting on the back of his chair. The men at the bar put down their bottles.

More than a minute went by before Howard looked over at Hubble. He had not heard him get up, but it was not this that made his hands tighten on the edge of the table as much as the expression on Hubble's face. His eyes were narrowed and his lips drawn back, not in a grimace, but as if suddenly all the air had been drained out of his lungs.

A moment later the soldier saw him. He guided Regal through a few more steps—like a mechanical toy running down—then stopped. He stood, still holding Regal in the dance position, looking over her shoulder at Hubble across the room. Then he released her and slowly walked to the far end of the bar, apart from the other men.

The song ended. The juke box clicked off and the room became silent. Hubble had not moved, nor had his expression changed. Regal stood in the center of the room with her back toward him. Her arms were at her sides, her shoulders bent. She turned to face the table. The lights played over her skirt and shoulders, but her face was in shadow; Howard could not see it. As he watched her Regal straightened slightly. The movement was barely perceptible, but it was enough to alter her whole being, to change her from something that was merely the recipient of Hubble's stare and the nervous looks of the others in the room, into someone who had not yet allowed herself to become merely the receptacle for whatever came her way. The girl isolated in the middle of the dark room was still the one who had been an inanimate object on the back seat of the Hudson and had climbed musty stairways to lie in a drunken stupor in a hundred hotel rooms. But this moment there was something about her that had not been there before—not a posture of defiance or planned escape but something inward.

Behind him Howard heard a chair scrape. As he turned to look, Hubble came out from behind the table and started toward Regal. He stopped, just on the edge of the dance floor. For more than a minute they stared at each other across a distance of twenty feet, each of them fixed yet buffeted by the swirling lights. Then Hubble turned away and headed out the door. Regal stood there a moment longer, then followed him. Before she had reached the door the soldier ran out to the center of the room, picked up her sweater and put it over her shoulders. Regal did not notice him.

When Howard came out the engine was running and the headlights were on. But Regal was standing by the front fender. Hubble was behind the wheel, his door open. Howard stopped a few feet from the car.

"What do you think?" Regal said.

Howard looked at Hubble, then Regal.

"That's right, I'm talking to you. I asked you a question."

"Well, I don't know what you're talking about. I don't think anything."

"You don't?" Regal hugged her arms. "That's pretty strange, if you ask me, because if I was you I'd be thinking about a lot of things. For instance, I'd be thinking about how it is he can sit around every night without blinking an eye while any old boy with five bucks and an itch puts it to me, and then tonight he sees me dancing with that G. I. and he can't handle it."

"Shut up!" Hubble said. "You keep your goddam mouth shut if you know what's good for you."

Regal moved around the fender closer to Howard. "You see, *he'd* never tell you, not in a million years. Maybe he doesn't even know. But I can tell you the reason if you're interested. After all, you got a right to know, seeing you're a part of it now."

The blue neon sign buzzed above them. "What do you mean, I'm part of it?"

"Nothing," Hubble said. "She don't mean nothing. So you just keep out of it."

"Something!" Regal screamed. She tore the sweater from her shoulders and threw it to the ground. "I mean a lot! I mean the only reason he keeps you around is so he won't ever get to thinking he's got anything on his hands except a five-dollar whore. He couldn't do it by himself. He couldn't do it if it was just him and me. You see what I mean, mister? He's got to use your eyes to see me, and I'm nothing to you but a whore."

Someone opened the front door of the roadhouse. Howard looked around. The door closed. "I didn't say that."

"Shut up! What do I care what you think about me! I'm talking about *him*, mister. I'm telling you he can just about pull it off if there's you or somebody like you along all the time. Just about, but not quite." Regal leaned against the side of the Hudson and began to laugh. "What you don't know is, there's some tears in those dry eyes of his. And I'm drinking them. You'd never believe they was there, would you? I mean, anybody would think that if he ever thought about me it'd be 'fuck the whore' he'd be thinking, and that'd be it. Yeah, well, that's the way he'd like it to be. It's what he wants more than anything, just to be able to say 'fuck the whore' and have done with it. But he can't do it quite. And if you want to know something else that'll surprise you, mister, I drink his tears every day in a couple of pints of whisky that somehow get into the back seat. I mean, it's better when I'm drunk—for me *and* him. But also, you see, sometimes he forgets he's supposed to be looking through somebody else's eyes. Like tonight he forgot, and you saw what happened."

"I told you to shut up!" Hubble got out of the front seat and slammed the door. "That's *all* you are to me, a five-buck whore; and that's all you ever been, so don't try to make something else out of it. And don't try to make it seem like *I'm* forgetting anything, sister, because I got a pretty good memory."

Regal walked over and stood in front of Howard. "You work in tough bars and you end up being a lot of things you never counted on. But *everybody* knew what I was. I didn't try to hide anything."

"Lying!" Hubble shouted. "Not everybody knew. She was fooling some people and laughing behind their back. She's trying to twist it now so it'll seem like she didn't know what was happening all the time."

"You see what's going on, mister? You see what it's all about?"

"You see shit!" Hubble moved to one side of Howard. "Maybe sometime you been made a sucker or been tricked out of something, but nobody's talking about that. I'm talking about something else, you know what I mean? When you're not looking for it. Otherwise you can do something about it. You drive a truck and you get a blowout at seventy-five miles an hour, you better be able to handle it. If you can't, it's your own goddam fault." Hubble wiped his forehead with his sleeve. "But, sonny, you tell me what to do when . . . ah shit!" His voice trailed off.

Regal poked Howard's shoulder. "There were truckers that used to stop. Part of what I was supposed to do in this place besides waiting on table was to be nice to these truckers so they'd keep coming back. I mean, this place was out in the middle of nowhere! How could you leave? How could you ever get away unless you got some money?"

Hubble nodded. "Yeah, get money by being nice to 'em. That's just the way it was."

"But even with all the truckers, he was the one you'd notice, the one that could just walk into any place, say what he wanted and end up getting it."

"I ended up getting a cheap whore. That's what I ended up getting."

Regal touched Howard's shoulder again. "Everybody *knew* what I was," she said softly. "So how come *he* didn't know? I'll tell you why—because it wasn't even me he was seeing. I was just something he wanted. He never even bothered to look close. Just wanting me was enough. Just getting me was all that mattered to him. There's worse things than me; I know there is. He was pretending I was something else, a girl of his dreams maybe. He never really saw me. I wasn't trying to fool anybody. How could I fool anybody? He was the one that was doing the fooling."

Howard walked over to the car. He stood with his back to them, looking over the hood to the dark highway. "Then why are you together?" he said. "You could leave."

Regal came up behind him. "No good. You don't know, do you? There's a reason."

"Then shut up! Shut up, both of you!" Howard shouted. He turned to face them. "I don't want to hear, don't you understand? I don't want to hear about it. It was better before, goddam you. It was better when it was nothing, when it was just one of you driving and the other in the back seat, and that was it. Because at least then there was nothing worse. It was as good as it could be and as bad at the same time, don't you understand? Don't you know what I'm talking about? There was no shit underneath, and there was no lying and no corny two-bit sob story, and now you ruined the whole thing. It's right back where it starts. You're playing games, goddam you both, and that's what you told me wasn't going to happen, Hubble. That's exactly what you said—that you didn't want to know what's going on inside my head and I wasn't about to know what was inside yours. And it would have been better, you were right, because what's going on in everybody's head is a lot of shit." He put a cigarette in his mouth, then snatched it out and threw it on the ground. *"Everybody,* everybody I ever knew, they're living their lives on top and they're dying underneath. I know they are. They're just keeping themselves alive with some stupid dreams they couldn't even handle if they came true. You were right and now I got to listen to all this stuff, so you fucking well better listen to me, Hubble. You know all that talk of yours about being free from everything that everybody else thinks about—being free from those men in Hargrett you said were dead before they were born? Well, listen, you're *in* it, you're in it worse than any of them because she's right; what kind of a man would sit around every night like you do? One that's in it so deep he's coming out the other side. And all that sick crap of sending stooges up to her every night doesn't mean a thing. You only got taken by yourself, that's all that happened. And you took me too because all those things you were telling me never did any good for you. They did nothing. You know where you belong? Right back in Hargrett with all those men I've been seeing all my life, and right with Miss Cowley, and . . . and what about *me,* goddam you, Hubble? I'm not in it at all. Do you know where that leaves me? *Do* you?" Inside the roadhouse someone was playing the juke box.

"I don't know what the hell you're talking about," Hubble said.

Howard took a step toward him and stopped. "You don't? You want to keep on with it then? Okay then, let's do it. Only let's do it the right way, huh? I mean, we might as well find out if we're all talking about the same thing. Don't you think so? Don't you both think so?" Howard moved next to Regal. He grabbed her hand. "There's a *lot* of stooges in there just waiting for somebody like her, right? So here's what we do, Hubble; you wait right here and she and I'll go back for a little visit. We'll just go back in, the two of us, and we'll let that soldier boy finish what he started; and when he's all done we'll start with all the stooges at the bar, and you stay here and wait for us because you're still running things, Hubble."

Regal did not resist as Howard led her up the walk toward

the front door. "You see what I mean," Howard said, "we might find out we're all talking about something different, and then we'd all three of us be right back where we started."

And then Hubble was there. He came out of the darkness into the blue light and stepped between Howard and Regal, breaking their grasp. For a moment they stood pressed against Hubble; then Howard moved back, and the three of them stood in a close circle. Regal was swaying. "You see?" she said softly. "You see what I was talking about?"

"Is that a fact?" Howard went down the walk to the car. He picked up Regal's sweater and put it on the hood. "Well, I'll be seeing you. I mean, wouldn't you say this is about it for the three of us? Wouldn't you say it's getting a little crowded in that Hudson about now?"

Hubble and Regal had not moved.

"I'm going to take the car, Hubble."

Hubble's head snapped up. He came part way down the walk. "You're going to take shit, sonny! What do you think, you and her just go through all this stuff and now everything's different? You think everybody's going to settle down some place and pick violets? Yeah, well, nothing's changed. You know what I'm going to do if I feel like it? I'm going to keep on doing just what's been going on, just as long as I feel like doing it, so you just mind your own goddam business."

"Give him the car," Regal said behind him. "Let him have it."

"You shut your fucking mouth!" Hubble screamed. He whirled around. His hand caught Regal in the side of the face. She stumbled backward.

Howard started toward them, then stopped. "What are you going to do then, start riding around again with her in the back seat? You think that's going to work? You going to find somebody else to take my place, is that it? That's what you're going to have to do, Hubble, find somebody to take my place." Now it was Howard who was shouting again. "You son of a bitch, you think you need the car more than I do? You think all I got to do is stick around and keep playing games with you? It's over, you understand, it's all over. I got things to do, you see? I got a lot of things to do. You see, you won, Hubble; you're a big winner, only you don't know it yet. I won the game for you, so I get the car, right? It's a big prize for me, right?"

Regal was close behind Hubble again. "Take it," she said. "Take the car and get out of here."

Howard's shoulders sagged. "What the hell difference does it make. You want the car? You can have it. It doesn't make any difference to me."

"Take it," Regal said. Hubble stood with his legs apart, staring at Howard.

Howard started back to the Hudson. He took Regal's sweater from the hood. "You've got enough money for a while." He reached into his pocket, took out a crumpled piece of paper and studied it in the faint light. "You've got almost fifty dollars." Neither of them answered. Howard held out Regal's sweater to her. He stood there for a long moment, his arm outstretched. Then he let the sweater drop.

He got into the Hudson and backed out onto the highway. He did not look at them again. Hubble still stood in the narrow path, with Regal behind him, using Hubble as a shield from the wind. Only when he was moving forward down the highway did he look in the rear view mirror, but he saw just the blue light growing smaller. He drove for only a few minutes, then pulled over onto the gravel, shaking so hard that his hands could barely control the wheel.

Again, on a cold night, boarding a long distance bus at two o'clock in the morning, you pull yourself up the step through the rubber-lipped telescoping door. You wait at the head of the aisle, both intruder and expected guest, not yet ready to enter the anonymity of darkness, holding back before you begin your walk between rows of huddled shapes, holding onto your aloneness for another moment before you give into the silent vacuum, the trapped warmth of shared breath. You follow the canopy of smoke threads, and there's not a word for you, not a turn of a head as you begin your walk. You are already known; they have finished their inspection and digested you into the belly of their carrier. And what does it matter that you, cock of the walk, have timed your entrance, measured your pace? No one cares about your obligatory glance, your ill-masked rooster search. What'll it be, that first empty seat, possibility of a divorcée nestled against the dark window? Housewife on a holiday? Sink down next to her and spend the night groping through clothing. But no, pass her by; take the risk because somewhere in back, yeah that's the ticket, somewhere in back there'll be a golden lonely girl waiting for you with soft words, and you'll fly through the cold night together into morning.

Except there's only one place left in back, and it's next to a fat guy spread out all over the seat, and that's all there is to it. Still a few soft movements up front, and mysterious sighs; and there's still the divorcée traveling alone, but it's too late for her. The bus pulls out and you're in place. Then, five minutes later, you don't want to believe that the fat guy jammed beside you has begun to snore.

In the first light of morning crepe-faced old folks being shuttled through their last years, expert at packing a canvas overnight bag sealed with a combination lock, holding a linen dress or serge trousers that will lose their wrinkles in a child's closet. "The kids can double up for the weekend; they won't mind a bit," the kids minding the dry clove smell, the stiff fragility, the watery eyes, the lack of novelty in old age. Old folks, expert at balancing a tunafish sandwich on one knee in a moving bus.

Across the aisle, a soldier sitting there trying with bitten tobacco-stained fingers to pinch a crease back into his sagging trousers. Head full of code—PX, MOS, ETO. In his back pocket an old picture of a young girl is pressed between cloudy plastic. Behind him last night's drunk sprawls across the seat in a rubber-jointed stupor. From up front now the sour scream of a baby. The bus smells like a yawn.

And then, Christ, she's coming down the aisle toward you,

heading for the rest room. It's the divorcée; you recognize her coat. A pig. Forty if she's a day. Her lipstick's chewed off, and her face is all puffed up from sleep and sticky from pressing against the leatherette headrest. Nobody can say you were ever that hard up. Still . . . at night in a dark bus. . . . You try a first cigarette and the smoke sticks in your throat.

The fat slob yawned and massaged his crotch. His shirt had spilled over his belt. "Don't let anybody ever tell you an accountant's got an easy life."

Crow nodded and tried to shift in his seat He was wedged.

"You know what time I finished with their books in Dawson? Eleven o'clock. That's eleven o'clock last night. You wanna know what time I started? *Two* o'clock, two o'clock in the afternoon. That's nine hours straight I was working on them books. I mean, I'm talking about nine straight hours without a break. Know what I had for supper? Two burgers and a Coca-Cola. That's all I had time for. Know what I'll be doing today? Working on somebody *else's* books. That's all you do when you're an accountant, balance somebody's books. You should see some of the deals I run into too; you wouldn't believe it. You know what? I can just look at a fellow's books and tell you the kind of person he is. It's a knack I got."

She was coming back from the rest room. Her lipstick was on straight now and her hair combed, and as she went by his seat Crow got a faint whiff of perfume. But one of her stockings was loose. As she went down the aisle it crimped on her calf like a little flap of skin.

Crow squirmed out of the seat. " 'Scuse me, I just saw a friend of mine." He touched the front of his pants an instant and started down the aisle.

" 'Scuse me. Is there anybody sitting here?" Crow leaned over the double seat, his eyes on a level with the top of her head. "I mean, there wasn't any room in back."

She turned from the window and looked up at him, surprised for only a moment. "No, I don't believe this seat *is* occupied."

"It's all full up in back." Crow lowered himself into the seat slowly, as if he were sitting on a carton of eggs. He sat as close to the aisle as possible and tried to look at her out of the corner of his eye without turning his head; but after a few minutes his eyes felt as if they would burst out of their sockets. He got a cigarette from his jacket pocket and a book of matches from his trousers, then held the cigarette and matches in his lap for five minutes before he asked, "You figure it's gonna bother you if I should happen to light up? Because, if it's gonna, it don't make that much difference to me if I light up or not." He could look at her as he spoke. She was maybe not quite forty, maybe between thirty-five and forty. There were lines in the corners of her eyes and running across her forehead, but they didn't bother him; she was sitting in the first sunlight of the day and nobody's face looked good when the sun was shining on it through a bus window. It didn't bother him, and she wasn't bad looking with her lipstick on straight and her hair combed. She had her coat pulled around her, so he couldn't get any idea of her breasts.

"No, it won't bother me."

"You sure? It don't make any difference to me if I have a cigarette."

She smiled. "Please. I don't mind."

Crow jabbed his hand into his jacket and pulled out the pack. "You care for a coffin nail?"

"No. Thank you. I don't smoke."

Crow lit his cigarette and blew the smoke away from her. He held the cigarette out in the aisle. "Well, I wish I was you. I mean, I wish I never started smoking. The only thing is, in my business you get kind of nervous, if you know what I mean, and smoking kind of helps you relax."

She turned toward him now, and Crow let his head rest against the seat. With his cigarette hand he pushed the lever that inclined the seat back a half-dozen inches. "What is it you do?" she asked.

Crow took a drag on the cigarette and breathed the smoke out through his nostrils before he answered. "Well, if you really want to know, I'm a test driver."

The divorcée shifted in her seat. "A test driver?"

"Yeah, that's right," Crow said. "You see, all the big companies, like General Motors and Ford and Chrysler, they bring out these new-model cars every year. I mean, not the ones that everybody *sees,* but the ones they're working on for ten years from now. Experimental models is what they call them. So they need somebody to see what they can do. You know, how fast they'll go, and how the brakes and steering works, and if they're safe. Then, if they find out anything's wrong with them, they got to work on them some more."

The divorcée nodded. "And that's what you do?"

"Yeah. I been doing it for a long time."

"Well, I must say that's a real interesting job. But I believe something like that must be pretty dangerous, isn't it? I know those car people take a lot of trouble making those cars the best they can, but couldn't something go wrong when you weren't expecting it?"

The bus slowed down, then stopped just behind an automobile that was pulled up on the road shoulder. An old man got out of the back seat and someone inside handed him a suitcase. The bus door hissed open and the old man boarded, stood for a moment at the head of the aisle, and started toward the back. Crow waited until he had gone by before he answered.

"Well, like I said, I been doing it for a long time. You get to go to a lot of places testing different cars. As a matter of fact, I'm just getting back from California right now. Hollywood."

The divorcée didn't answer right away. She pulled the window shade down halfway to get the sun out of her eyes. "I see. Well, that sure is a fine job. And just think, here you are riding a bus."

Crow dropped his cigarette and stepped on it. "Yeah, I know. A lot of people don't understand that. But the thing is, I get tired driving all the time, so when I gotta go some place, like on a trip, I like to take it easy and kinda lay off driving for a while. You know, like the man says, leave the driving to us. I guess it's something like an airplane pilot when he . . . well, I mean, what is it *you* do? You do any kind of work?"

The divorcée smiled and folded her hands in her lap. Then she leaned closer to Crow. "Yes, I do." She cleared her throat. "I guess you might say I do the Lord's work."

Crow nodded. "Is that a fact?"

"You see, I'm Ladies' Organizational Secretary for the Second Baptist Church Council of Bell County."

Crow reached for his cigarettes. "Is that a fact?"

"Yes, it is. I do quite a bit of traveling myself. For instance, right now I'm on my way to a meeting of the Southeastern Texas Planning Congress."

"Right," Crow said.

She smiled. "What's the church of *your* faith, if I could ask?"

"Yeah, well, you see lately I been doin' a lot of traveling like I told you."

The divorcée crossed her legs. "Could I ask you if you ever pray to Jesus Christ for assistance in time of need or uncertainty?"

Crow leaned out into the aisle and scanned the seats behind him. The old man was pinned in next to the slob. "Yeah, I do that a lot, as a matter of fact. I want to say it's been a real pleasure talking to you like this. The thing is, I ain't had no sleep for about three days running now, so I figure maybe I'll take a little nap and kinda catch up while I got the chance, if you know what I mean, ma'am." He pushed the seat back farther and closed his eyes.

The divorcée touched his arm. "Would you join me in a prayer? Just a short one. I believe it might even help you sleep a little more peacefully. It always works for me."

Crow didn't answer.

"Well, would you mind if *I* said a little prayer? You could listen, and that'd be almost the same as if you were praying along with me. I mean, you got to crawl before you can walk."

She cleared her throat. "Dear God, listen we beseech You to the prayers of Your humble servants, us poor sinners who every day stumble farther down the road of wickedness and sin. Teach us to abandon our lives of slothfulness and deceit and prepare ourselves for the everlasting rewards of the Kingdom of Heaven. Help us to denounce the temptations that men set before us, and assist us to follow the only true example, our Lord Jesus Christ, who came onto this earth to help us get rid of our sins. Make us strong enough, we ask You, to follow His way."

Yeah, well, where were they now? Out cruising around somewhere in his car, that's where they were; laughing at him while he's stuck on this goddam bus, and telling everybody they meet how they took this poor sucker for his car. They'd probably wrecked it by now anyway. Sure as shit the car's not worth a nickel any more. As if they'd even think about taking it in for a check-up. And it was due for one too, about three weeks ago, a major one. Suppose they took it to some jerk who didn't know what he was doing? That's what they'd do too, some guy who wouldn't even know how to mix the oil right or file down the bushings. It wouldn't make any difference to them. They didn't spend any two years fixing it up so it purred like a kitten. It was a sweet car and it was his car, and they stole it and they wrecked it and right now they were laughing about it.

"Dear God, we are all sinners, but You have made us in Your image and put us a little lower than the angels. Help us through the divine grace of our Lord Jesus Christ to pattern our lives like His life, staying on the path of goodness and righteousness and knowing that whatever we put our heart and soul to we will accomplish, so long as it goes along with the teachings of our Lord Jesus Christ. Dear God, help this young man to cleanse his soul and face the future with a pure heart, secure in the knowledge that whatever he does You are close by, waiting to be his guide if only he will call on You. Let him find Your always-present Being and go forward into the future with the confidence and dedication that only faith in You can bring about."

Crow put his hand inside his pants. Well, he'd get 'em. They could laugh now, but they wouldn't be doing too much laughing after a while. It'd be just when they didn't expect it—that's when he'd find 'em. And they could talk all they wanted to and promise him anything under the sun, and they could see how far that'd get 'em. Because he'd just be standing there nice and loose, watching 'em squirm and listening to 'em make all the promises they could think of. Then everybody would find out who was running things.

Howard awoke, cold. His knees were jammed under the steering wheel. The door handle pressed against his cheek. His feet were stiff with cold. He twisted in the seat so that he was lying on his back, and pulled Regal's sheet up around him. Through the windshield the morning was wool gray; clouds broke apart as they raced across the sky. The car seemed to be turning, as if the wind that rattled the windows was spinning it. He listened, and there was nothing but the wind, and it was as if there was not much time: as if he could not hold out for long, sealed inside the automobile, before the wind penetrated, at first through a crack in the rear window or up between the floor boards or through the radiator grill; a little trickle of air on the back of his neck at first, then growing stronger, strong enough to whisper up the sand and dust off the floor, then, cracking a window, shattering it, roaring into the car until all the windows exploded, pulling off the doors to get at him and send him a hundred miles across the desert in sprawling cartwheels. He closed his eyes.

When he opened them again the sky was tinted with red and the wind had lowered in pitch. He sat up slowly inside the sheet and stamped his feet until they began to tingle. He lit a cigarette and held it with two fingers poking through the sheet. Ahead, the unbroken stretch of macadam was slick under a coat of morning frost. The desert scrub was cold and stiff, unbending to the wind, and all around the car the earth followed the sky to distant horizons; the car was beneath the center of a cloud canopy, a hemisphere inflated by the rushing wind. He slid behind the wheel and switched on the ignition. The gears screamed as he shifted into first and edged out onto the highway.

Ten minutes later he drove into Weldon. Chains of lightbulbs arched over the main street, which was empty except for a few automobiles parked along a concrete mall. He drove past the Greyhound station where two gleaming buses waited shoulder to shoulder. At one end of the square, on the courthouse lawn, a fifteen-foot wooden cowboy with a Santa Claus cap and drawn six shooters stood inside a ring of white Christmas trees.

He pulled over to the curb and got out. But first he took Hubble's dark glasses from the glove compartment and put them on. The sheet trailed along the sidewalk as he walked over to the wooden bench on the edge of the lawn and sat down. The December sun was rising now at the end of Main Street; sunlight reflected off the roofs of the parked cars and the windows of the squat wooden stores lining two sides of the square. Somewhere in Weldon a truck moved through the streets, starting up, accelerating, slowing, starting again. It appeared now in the far corner of the square, a faded blue flat-nosed pick-up with cages of full and empty milk bottles stacked behind the cab. The driver's arm rested on the window frame. The truck turned off the square and disappeared around the side of the Baxter Hotel, and the sound of its engine trailed off. Next to the bench a trickle of water from the mouth of a drinking fountain gurgled in the drain of the porcelain bowl. The cowboy creaked in the wind. A soft hollow bone rattle came from the lightbulb strings.

Howard got up. He stood in front of the Hudson, holding the sheet together at his chest with one hand. There were pock marks of rust dotting the chrome grill. The lips of the radiator guard were encrusted with insect bodies. In the streaked windshield he could see the cowboy towering behind him. He began to walk. The wind blew papers and dust across his path as he walked slowly around the square past shops whose doors were barred with iron lattices. In a dark window a chalky soldier in full-dress uniform looked out at the square. His left hand was missing; the sleeve was stuffed with newspaper. In front of the store next to the soldier's a dozen silver garbage cans were chained together through their handles, the end of the chain padlocked to the bars of the cellar window. In an alley a motorcycle half covered by white oilcloth was chained through four truck tires. In another window a cat slept with its back flattened against the glass, and above it shreds of yellow chicken skin stuck to a row of hanging hooks. There were benches all along the line of stores. Under them were piles of cigarette and cigar butts. A folded newspaper stuck out from the slotted back of one bench. A blue sweater was tied to the arm of another. At the corner of the square there were lights on behind the steamy windows of a café. Howard stopped in front of the window and looked around. The cowboy was blocked from view by a hanging banner advertising the Christmas Day rodeo, but he could hear it creaking. He turned away and went into the café.

It was empty. The dark plastic counter showed the streaks of a wet rag. The pastry case and the mirror behind the counter were clouded with steam that hissed from a stainless-steel coffee urn. A black iron hood hung above the polished griddle. Someone was moving in the back of the café, and in a moment an old Mexican woman in a black dress and shawl came through a door on one side of the counter. She stopped when she saw Howard. They stared at each other across the counter for almost a minute, then Howard took off the sheet, rolled it up and dropped it on the floor, and sat down. The old woman stayed in the doorway, then edged through and stood on the far side of the coffee urn. Howard took off the dark glasses and lit a cigarette. He took only two drags before he snuffed it out. The urn was hissing loudly now. The old woman reached around it and turned a knob. Without looking away from Howard she got a coffee mug from under the counter and filled it. She held the mug in both hands for a moment, then walked over and set it in front of Howard and moved back to the urn. She leaned forward and pulled the shawl about her neck. "Soldier?" she whispered. Howard nodded. "Soldier," she said.

She moved over in front of the griddle and watched him drink his coffee. When he had finished she took his cup and filled it again, then went over and sat down in a small rocking chair by the front window, and began to rock slowly, her back to him. There were bells ringing in the square now, the sour one-note clang of the courthouse bell mingling with the chimes of a church. When they had stopped the old woman got up and began to set places on the counter. She did not look at Howard again, and she had disappeared through the door when he got up, put a quarter next to his mug and went out, leaving the sheet on the floor.

The square was empty. He stood in front of the café for a moment and headed for the Hudson. He was halfway across the square when he stopped, rubbed his eyes, then cut back toward the hotel.

He went up the stairs, pushed open the glass door, and went into the lobby. The room was lit by two giant fluorescent lights hanging by chains from the ceiling. Against one wall a dozen metal chairs were stacked, legs up, on a table. A rusty soda machine stood next to the stairway at the back. The room clerk was sitting in a wicker chair behind the registration counter, his face hidden by a magazine. He did not look up as Howard walked toward him, and he continued to read when Howard was standing in front of the desk. A minute went by before he lowered the magazine, folded it carefully, and slid it into a mail slot behind him. His long narrow horse jaw was patched with gray stubble. His hair, white at the roots and the color of brown shoe polish at the edges, was parted down the center of his skull, curling in little wisps at his temples. His jowels quivered as he worked a toothpick back and forth across his mouth. "I know you," he said.

"I've been here before."

The clerk leaned back and touched the toothpick. "Yeah, I know that. I seen you here before. Where's your friends? Where's your traveling companions?"

Howard rubbed his toe against the desk. "Look, have you got a room? I'd like to get some sleep, if you know what I mean."

"What'd they do, ditch you, son? I bet they did. You want to know something? It don't surprise me none. I could tell just by looking at 'em they was going to ditch you when the mood hit 'em. Leave you in the lurch, did they? Probably didn't leave you with a lot of money either, I'll bet." He grinned. The toothpick was wedged between two front teeth.

"I've got enough to pay for the room, if that's what's worrying you."

The clerk leaned forward and rested his elbows on the desk. "Don't worry none about the room, son. You just wait a minute; let me tell you something. I got something you just might be interested in." He glanced over his shoulder at the stairway, then pulled his chair closer to the desk. "Now look, this is a soldier town, right? Five or six hundred G. I.s in town every Saturday night, right? *More* than that probably, more than a thousand. Even on your week night they'll be a few hundred in town. I know that for a fact, in case you're interested, because I been paying attention lately. Okay, now listen to this. You don't need that fella and his girl no more, because what I'm saying is you and me can work out something a whole lot better than anything you had going with them. You follow me?" He took the toothpick from his mouth, examined it, and fitted it back into the slot. "Look, can we get another little girl? Hell, two or *three* little girls while we're at it. I mean, think about it; the hotel's no problem. I can work any shift I want, long as I tell 'em a couple of days ahead. Don't make any difference to the other fella either because he's an old man. So all *you* got to do is get the little girls, right? I'm telling you, son, it'll be an awful lot better than that setup you was working before. Just think about it; the room won't cost us nothing. What do you think?"

Howard nodded. "It's fine. It's just perfect. Do you think I could have that room now?"

The clerk didn't answer him. One side of his face was twitching. He rose from the wicker chair as if he had been pulled up by a string. The toothpick dropped to the desk. "What is this?"

he said softly. "What's it you're trying to pull here?" He was not looking at Howard. He was looking beyond him. Howard turned.

It was Crow. He stood just inside the glass door. His leather jacket was buttoned to the neck, the fur collar turned up. He held the revolver close to his stomach with both hands. For an instant he looked behind him out the door, then took a couple of steps forward and stopped directly under one of the fluorescent lights. He ran his tongue over his lips. "All right now, like the man says, just don't neither of y'all move at all. Hear what I'm saying? Y'all just stay exactly where you are."

Howard's spine was against the desk. Behind him, the clerk froze, his mouth open.

Crow stood there in the center of the room, frowning as if he could not think of what to say next. He looked at Howard.

"Hello, hoss," Howard said.

Crow grinned. "Hi, Howie. How you doin'?"

"Not bad. You?"

The grin disappeared. "Look, Howie, nobody's saying I got anything against you. I know how he operates, and I know how he probably fast talked you into going along with him same as he did me. All this time it's been him and her I been after, not you. I mean, you're still a buddy of mine, Howie, same as before. That's the truth."

"I appreciate that, Crow. That's the truth too."

"Yeah, well, Howie, that don't mean you should try anything. I mean, the best thing you can do is stay where you are until I settle things with them." Crow was breathing hard.

"What about me?" The desk clerk's adam's apple bobbed up and down as he spoke. "I don't know anything about any of this. My wife's waiting for me right now. This is between you and him."

"You shut up!" Crow screamed. "You just stay where you are and don't try anything or you'll be wishing you hadn't." He wiped the sweat off his forehead with the back of his hand. The hand holding the .45 was shaking. He quickly braced it again. "Where they at, Howie? They upstairs with somebody?"

Howard sighed. "Is it all right if I light up a cigarette, Crow?"

"It's all right, Howie, but I'm not fooling around; you better believe it. Maybe nobody ever figured they'd see me again, is that it?" His voice was higher pitched than it had been. "You think maybe I didn't know what you was all up to right from the start? Yeah, well, I knew. I never believed anything, because I had it figured right from the start that he was trying to play me for a sucker and the only thing he cared about was my car." Sweat was streaming down the sides of Crow's face now. His hair was plastered to his forehead. "I was just going along with him and her till I got my chance, that's all. You must've thought I was pretty stupid, didn't you? Well, I'm not, you can count on that. Nobody puts anything over on me, and you was all just lucky back there that I had my mind on something else at the moment. But nobody's lucky now because I'm here, ain't I? I caught up with you, and that's something nobody ever took into account."

The clerk raised one hand. "I just wanted to tell you there's gonna be people coming in here soon."

"Howie?" Crow said.

Howard blew out a stream of smoke. "They're not here, Crow. I'm here alone."

Crow took a step backward and looked from Howard to the clerk. "What are you saying, Howie?"

"I got the car, Crow, so you can have it. They're not here."

"That's right," the clerk said. "There's nobody here."

"What are you saying, Howie? Where are they?"

"I don't know where they are. You can have the car. That's what you want, isn't it?"

Crow stepped back again. "I can *have* it? It's my car. You think you're going to *give* it to me, is that it? What was you going to do, Howie? You left 'em. What did you think you were going to do with the car? I want to know. You better tell me."

Howard stepped on his cigarette. "I don't know. I just got here."

"Yeah? Well, I just got here too, didn't I? Maybe I got here just in time, if you know what I mean. What's going on, Howie?"

"Nothing's going on. The car's all right."

Crow wiped his forehead again. "Yeah, you just said that, Howie. You just left 'em. Maybe what you did was pull a fast one on 'em, is that what you did? I mean, how come all of a sudden you just left 'em after all this time?" The .45 was shaking.

Howard didn't answer.

The desk clerk cleared his throat. "Would it be all right if I lit up a cigarette too?"

"I gotta *do* something!" Crow shouted. "You think I'm just gonna drive off and not do nothing after all this time? You understand what I'm saying, Howie? I come all this way and all this time and now you're telling me all there is to do is just get in the car and drive off. Well listen, I gotta *do* something!"

The clerk had taken a cigarette from his pocket, but he did not light it.

"It don't work that way," Crow said. "Somebody don't drive off with my car and keep it all this time and then when they're all through with it just give it back to me and tell me everything's all right. It *ain't* all right! It ain't all right till I say it is. What about all that time y'all been driving around thinking you pulled a fast one on me? I'm telling you, Howie, something's gonna happen." The leather jacket was streaked with sweat. "Just don't try anything. I'm warning you, Howie, just don't try to pull anything, because I'm handling things now."

Howard's palms were flat against the desk behind him. He spoke slowly. "Okay, Crow, you're handling things. Take it easy. You got the car, right? And that's what you came for. Just take it easy, Crow. You don't *have* to get back at anybody any more because you've got the car. Anything else and you'll just get into a lot of trouble. That's the truth, hoss, you know that."

"He's right," the clerk whispered. "He's absolutely right."

Crow stared at Howard. He made a choking sound in his throat. Then his shoulders slumped. "For crying out loud,

Howie, what kind of trouble can I get in? It ain't even loaded." His arms dropped to his sides. The .45 dangled from his trigger finger.

"It ain't loaded!" the clerk shouted. He looked from Crow to Howard, then bolted for the stairs and raced up out of sight.

Howard rested against the desk for several seconds before he walked over to Crow who was standing with his head bowed. "We better get out of here, hoss. He'll be calling the police probably." He put his hand on Crow's shoulder.

Crow nodded slowly. "Okay, Howie. Let's go."

They went out the glass door onto the porch. "We better not run," Howard said. "We don't want to attract any attention." But it was he who began to run as soon as they reached the bottom of the steps. They ran across the center of the square, past a corridor of parking meters, past a bronze plaque with a wreath of flowers wired to its base, past the Christmas rodeo sign.

The bells began to ring just before they reached the car. Howard got behind the wheel and Crow jumped in next to him, and they drove out of town under the strings of rattling bulbs as the first group of people in Sunday clothes strolled into one corner of the square.

December nights, along the cold blacktop road that heads out of Del Rio northeast to San Antonio, men sit around battered wooden tables in filling stations in Bentonville, Cutter, Verdes, Wanger Corners. Twill jackets unzipped, boots on an oily stone floor smeared with tobacco strands, red- and black-checkered wool caps with last summer's hunting button pinned over an ear. Coal stove in a corner. Under the table on a chipped white piano stool, a fifth of Seven Crowns in a brown paper bag. TCU basketball game score from a grease-fingered white plastic radio. Remembering Merle Henderson, Charlie Henderson's boy. Had all the shots you need, and that's a fact. Game against

Tech, Merle won it with two foul shots after the buzzer, and I seen it. Put 'em both in with everybody watching him, maybe six, seven thousand people watching him, and that's pressure work, you better believe it. Could've made the pros, could've played ball with the pros any day of the week. Never did though, did he? Where'd he end up anyway, Merle Henderson? Sand in the wind ticking against the plate-glass window. Cold. Hell, it ain't the weather, it's gettin' old that's botherin' you. Like the man said, it ain't the cold, it's the *old*. That's a fact too. I believe you couldn't raise it up if that Gina what's-her-name on the TV last night walked in here through that front door right this minute and set herself right down on this table. Think so, do you? Well, boy, I'm telling you one thing, she walks in here and you better clear a path for me 'cause I'll be comin' through. Tell you one thing, he won't be raisin' it if his old lady gets wind of it. Won't have nothin' left to raise. Hell, she'd liable to die out of surprise. She's been tryin' to raise it up for the last ten years now. That's the truth. Fella drives in here this afternoon comin' from the north, wantin' to know how far he's gotta go before he gets to Coppraston. So I tell him if he keeps right on straight like he's doin' he could figure on maybe fifty thousand miles or so before he pulled into Coppraston, but if he turns himself around he oughta hit it in about seven miles. Fella lookin' for Coppraston to be south, was he? Drove right through it without knowin' the difference. Figured on sneakin' up behind it, did he? Hey! Customer out there!

The Hudson waited by a pump.

"Fill it for you?"

"Take a look at the water too. Don't have to bother with the oil. This automobile don't burn no oil." The orange bubble in the pump whirled to bells.

"That'll be three dollars even. Out of five. Thank you. Used to have one of these old cars myself."

"Yeah? Well, I got one now." The Hudson gunned out of the station.

"Runs pretty good though, don't she? You gotta admit that."

Crow took a swallow of beer and handed the can to Howard.

"It sure does. It's a real great car."

"Yeah, well, it ought to be. I sure put enough time into it." Crow giggled. "Hey, that ol' boy was pretty scared, right? Figured I was gonna shoot him in the ass any minute."

Howard dropped the beer can out the window. "Can't say I blame him too much, hoss."

"Shit, I knew what I was doing. Think I was going to bother shooting anybody and ending up in jail? I was just trying to scare you a little is all. You knew that all along, Howie." Crow wiped his nose. "Figure the police are looking for us?"

"I don't know. Nobody was hurt."

"Yeah, that's right, nobody was hurt. Well, how much money you got left, Howie?"

Howard reached into his pocket and took out some bills. He held them close to the dashboard lights. "About fourteen dollars. How about you?"

"Maybe ten. Got any idea what you want to do?"

"I don't know. Let's keep going north for a while, just in case anyone *is* looking for us."

"You figuring to stop back in Hargrett, Howie?"

Howard lit a cigarette before he answered. "I don't know. I haven't thought about it."

"We could always join up. I talked to a lot of army guys, and they say it ain't too bad. A lot of these guys say that one thing about being in the army is you get to know all the places to go to get laid." Crow looked over at Howard. "I mean, other things too."

"Yeah, well, why don't we just keep driving for a while and see what happens. Maybe we'll get out of Texas for a while."

"Get out of Texas?"

"I'm just thinking about it. I've never been."

"You want to drive for a while?" Crow pulled over to the side of the road and climbed into the back seat. In a minute Howard had the Hudson up to seventy-five.

"Howie?" Crow spoke from the darkness of the back seat.

"One thing I was wondering about. Like I said, I know how good Hubble was at fast talking people into doing things, but I was wondering what he could've said to you that day in the bus. I mean, you and me been buddies for a long time and you didn't even know him. I didn't figure you'd take off like that and leave me waiting. I mean, Howie, I was hanging around that bus for two days, till I just knew nobody was coming back."

Howard pulled into the left lane to pass a slow-moving truck. "I don't know what to tell you, Crow."

"Shit, you don't have to tell me *nothing* if you don't want. I been screwed up myself sometimes, if you want to know the truth. I just figured something important was going on, like him maybe forcing you to go with him."

"Okay, Crow, listen. You take me out to that bus, and there's Hubble waiting there, and he's a real big man, right? The girl didn't have anything to do with it; she was just there. It was Hubble, do you know what I'm talking about, Crow? I never saw anyone like Hubble before. You got the feeling he could handle anything that came along. And you got the feeling he knew exactly where he was going, and it didn't even make any difference where as long as *he* knew. That's all there was to it. There was nothing about ditching you. All I was thinking about was sticking with him for a while."

"Yeah," Crow said, "I gotta admit that about him. He handled himself pretty well. The thing is, I got the car back. That's the only thing that was bothering me."

For a minute neither of them spoke, listening to the rushing wind and the steady hum of the tires. Then Crow said in a sleepy voice, "Maybe it's kind of like me looking for y'all with an empty gun."

"That's what it's like, Crow."

"Okay, Howie."

For an hour Howard drove gripping the wheel tightly with both hands, watching the headlights skip over the broken white center strip, waiting with each mile for the triangular intersection that would split the highway, unable to think of why he should either turn off or continue on. There was no change in the road, no curve or stretch of pavement that became a landmark of the past. Somewhere now, not too far from the highway, must be an abandoned bus and after that a town, a house, a room, all strung out in front of him. Only time changed, and as the minutes went by the road seemed to climb. What was it they used to tell Billy Pendleton? That when you left Hargrett driving south it was all downhill, and once you got up a little speed you could switch off the ignition and coast the rest of the way; but if you didn't pay attention you'd roll right into the Gulf of Mexico. And all the gas stations were on the left side of the highway because driving back up north it was all uphill.

And then it was there, expected, yet sudden. He swerved sharply. The skeleton of a barn was leaning into the wind. Near it, on narrow rusted stilts, a man in top hat and formal dress smoked a cigar. White crosses against the sky marked a slash of railroad track. Slowing down the Hudson now—fifty, forty, thirty—as the blacktop widened into white cement patched yellow under the streetlights. The town was fixed in an hour after midnight. On the far side of Mason's used-car lot the high school held the full moon in its windows. The courthouse, Wyandotte's courthouse, Weldon's courthouse, now Hargrett's courthouse, was dappled in shadow.

He drove through town slowly, picking out the clock in old man Temple's hardware store, the orange light in the drugstore cigar case. Down the block, Miss Cowley's house was dark.

Then out on the other side of town, out on the road where he had left his father not long enough ago to be a memory, past Boyd's garage, its asphalt yard swept clean, column of white pumps scrubbed and glistening. Over the concrete bridge of winter-dry Asino Creek, and it was not a return, but only a retracing of a road which even when first taken had no direction.

And that was why when he pulled onto the edge of the dirt yard it was only from habit, not because this moment was a moment apart, and why nothing had changed, nothing looked different. And yet he could feel his breath catching in his throat, feel the tightening in his chest. He sat in the car until the cigarette had burned down to his fingers, then he got out.

He stood in the yard. The moon was behind the house, outlining it; and he felt himself to be inside the house, felt his mother and father in the next room, Laura down the hall. He walked to the sagging barbed-wire fence over tire gouges made in last spring's rain. The tractor still lay on its back beyond the fence, its wheels pointing skyward. He looked around the yard. The truck was gone. Somewhere in the night, then, his father was driving down a deserted stretch of highway.

Or had they all gone? Was the house empty? It made no difference, because he was here, still with them and not just tonight, not just on a night of return; he was with them because he had never left. Nothing had changed because he had not changed. He was home safe; and, if he had found no choice between this house and the hotel room of a twisted pimp and a drunken prostitute, he could stay here and make no other choice.

He backed away from the fence. He could go up the porch steps, open the door, go softly up the stairs to his room. In the morning it would be as if nothing had happened between a summer night when he had run from his father and a winter night on which he had come back.

The house creaked in the wind. Howard held his breath. His legs felt for an instant as if they would not support him. He closed his eyes. The wind was at his back, flattening his jacket against him. He turned and headed into the wind toward the car.

Crow had not waked. Howard pulled the car slowly out onto the highway.

In the morning sunlight slanted across the front of the house and in through the bedroom window. It seemed to her, standing by the window, that this would be the last time she would ever wait for anything. But it was only a feeling, not really a thought, because she knew that the real waiting had just begun, or at least just begun to be recognized. Only, today was a special day, perhaps the last special day; and perhaps that was why she had been at the window for nearly an hour, though it was only eight o'clock and Boyd was not due to come for her until nine-thirty. How, then, should she take her leave? Was there a ritual she should be carrying out right now, going from room to room? But there was nothing to leave. It had all left her. And that wasn't it either; not the aloneness, but that the aloneness had come too late and she had no use for it. No use the quiet realization that she was glad Jess was dead, the memories sorted out and selected until she was able to create the same myth that Jess had held onto while alive—the good man failed, the luck run out. It is never the memories that hurt, unless we want them to. Not the stories made of lies and truth that we carefully prepare in advance to use when we need them. The only change in death is among the living, and it is all a trick that lasts only a short time. The footstep on the stair, which we have heard for twenty-five years, we hear again after it is gone. We sleep for a while on one side of the bed and wait for the sound of a truck or automobile pulling into the yard. Not the memories that hurt us; they are only blind ideas that tell us what we want to know.

It is only new answers to old reflexes that can surprise us and bring loneliness. Expecting to see and hear and touch for a moment what is gone, we learn the truth, not that someone has gone but that something has changed. And it is no good when the change becomes familiar and we are too old to be alone.

It was kind of Boyd to drive her, and a kind invitation of Burt and Laura's. But she would not stay for long; she would not stay always. Not a room at the back, dishes in a new sink, considerate retreats when moments of love or anger excluded her. What then? One room somewhere in the city, three flights up with Jesse's cowhide cutout of Texas on the wall? Cactus in a window box? Some kind of work behind a counter? Sunday dinner with the grandchild, and Burt's money pressed into her hand on leaving?

But how could it be a grandchild already? It was as if her

own children had become transparent, Laura absorbed into another person, someone's wife, someone's mother. Howard gone. They were like mirrors whose reflecting surface was wearing away so that she could see herself both in the reflection and on the other side. She would travel right through her children and see herself on the other side. Her generation was her grandchild's. Born again through the death of her husband and the disappearance of her children. But born too old, too old to be alone.

She would have another look then. She would walk through the house once more, pause in each room, find a memory to make it seem that it was more than an empty room with streaks of dust on its windows, furniture scratches on its floor. But it would just be doing something she felt was expected of her. The house had already disappeared.

About Harry Atkins

Harry Atkins is in his early thirties. While in the Army, he was stationed in Texas. He is now an editor for the New York Academy of Sciences, and lives with his wife in New York. He is well into a second novel.